Kate's magnificent brown eyes widened as her suspicions blossomed. "You broke in, didn't you?"

"I didn't break anything. I simply unlocked the door."

As if her knees had suddenly given way, she collapsed in a chair in front of her desk. "You broke into my room at home, too, didn't you? *You* ruined my study."

"No, Kate, I swear—"

Heartbreak glistened in her eyes. "Why should I believe anything you say? You've lied to me about everything, haven't you?"

"Not everything. I—"

"I'm calling security." She shoved to her feet, hands shaking.

He pushed the phone across the desk toward her. "Go ahead. They'll come and take me away. Then you'll never hear my side of the story."

She tilted her chin in a defiant angle. "Why should I care?"

"Because what we shared last night *wasn't* a lie."

"It was only a kiss. It didn't mean anything," she insisted.

He didn't believe her  and say that?"

Dear Reader,

Writing *Lover Under Cover* was a special pleasure
for me because I enjoyed creating the story of two
people who have suffered tragedy and disappointment
but manage to pick themselves up and go on to
ultimately find the love that they thought they'd
lost forever. Private investigator and cowboy hunk
Dean Harding is on a mission to reunite a missing
mother with her baby and the baby's father, but even
the experienced detective is unprepared for the surprises
that await him when he goes undercover at the Purvis
boardinghouse in Austin. Fate has plans for these
reluctant lovers, and sparks of attraction fly at their
first meeting. Like the irresistible force meeting an
immovable object, something's got to give! Kate
and Dean's story is a testament to the healing power
of love, and I hope you enjoy this installment of the
TRUEBLOOD, TEXAS story as much as I've enjoyed
writing it. I hope also that you'll look for my other
books in the Harlequin Intrigue and Harlequin American
Romance series.

Charlotte Douglas

TRUEBLOOD, TEXAS

Charlotte Douglas

Lover Under Cover

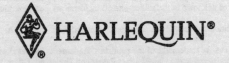

HARLEQUIN®

TORONTO • NEW YORK • LONDON
AMSTERDAM • PARIS • SYDNEY • HAMBURG
STOCKHOLM • ATHENS • TOKYO • MILAN • MADRID
PRAGUE • WARSAW • BUDAPEST • AUCKLAND

Charlotte Douglas is acknowledged
as the author of this work.

HARLEQUIN BOOKS
225 Duncan Mill Road, Don Mills,
Ontario, Canada M3B 3K9

ISBN 0-373-65092-2

LOVER UNDER COVER

Copyright © 2001 by Harlequin Books S.A.

Visit us at www.eHarlequin.com

Printed in U.S.A.

TRUEBLOOD TEXAS

THE TRUEBLOOD LEGACY

THE YEAR WAS 1918, and the Great War in Europe still raged, but Esau Porter was heading home to Texas.

The young sergeant arrived at his parents' ranch northwest of San Antonio on a Sunday night, only the celebration didn't go off as planned. Most of the townsfolk of Carmelita had come out to welcome Esau home, but when they saw the sorry condition of the boy, they gave their respects quickly and left.

The fever got so bad so fast that Mrs. Porter hardly knew what to do. By Monday night, before the doctor from San Antonio made it into town, Esau was dead.

The Porter family grieved. How could their son have survived the German peril, only to burn up and die in his own bed? It wasn't much of a surprise when Mrs. Porter took to her bed on Wednesday. But it was a hell of a shock when half the residents of Carmelita came down with the horrible illness. House after house was hit by death, and all the townspeople could do was pray for salvation.

None came. By the end of the year, over one hundred souls had perished. The influenza virus took those in the prime of life, leaving behind an unprecedented number of orphans. And the virus knew no boundaries. By the time the threat had passed, more than thirty-seven million people had succumbed worldwide.

But in one house, there was still hope.

Isabella Trueblood had come to Carmelita in the late 1800s with her father, blacksmith Saul Trueblood, and her mother, Teresa Collier Trueblood. The family had traveled from Indiana, leaving their Quaker roots behind.

Young Isabella grew up to be an intelligent woman who had a gift for healing and storytelling. Her dreams centered on the boy next door, Foster Carter, the son of Chester and Grace.

Just before the bad times came in 1918, Foster asked Isabella to be his wife, and the future of the Carter spread was secured. It was a happy union, and the future looked bright for the young couple.

Two years later, not one of their relatives was alive. How the young couple had survived was a miracle. And during the epidemic, Isabella and Foster had taken in more than twenty-two orphaned children from all over the county. They fed them, clothed them, taught them as if they were blood kin.

Then Isabella became pregnant, but there were complications. Love for her handsome son, Josiah, born in 1920, wasn't enough to stop her from growing weaker by the day. Knowing she couldn't leave her husband to tend to all the children if she died, she set out to find families for each one of her orphaned charges.

And so the Trueblood Foundation was born. Named in memory of Isabella's parents, it would become famous all over Texas. Some of the orphaned children went to strangers, but many were reunited with their families. After reading notices in newspapers and church bulletins, aunts, uncles, cousins and grandparents rushed to Carmelita to find the young ones they'd given up for dead.

Toward the end of Isabella's life, she'd brought together more than thirty families, and not just her orphans. Many others, old and young, made their way to her doorstep, and Isabella turned no one away.

At her death, the town's name was changed to Trueblood, in her honor. For years to come, her simple grave was adorned with flowers on the anniversary of her death, grateful tokens of appreciation from the families she had brought together.

Isabella's son, Josiah, grew into a fine rancher and married Rebecca Montgomery in 1938. They had a daughter, Elizabeth Trueblood Carter, in 1940. Elizabeth married her neighbor William Garrett in 1965, and gave birth to twins Lily and Dylan in 1971, and daughter Ashley a few years later. Home was the Double G ranch, about ten miles from Trueblood proper, and the Garrett children grew up listening to stories of their famous great-grandmother, Isabella. Because they were Truebloods, they knew that they, too, had a sacred duty to carry on the tradition passed down to them: finding lost souls and reuniting loved ones.

CHAPTER ONE

"NOBODY PROMISED YOU a rose garden," Kate Purvis muttered beneath her breath. "If you want one, you'll have to plant it yourself."

The scent of roses would be a pleasant change from the smell of antiseptic and disinfectants that clung to her clothes and hair, even once she'd left the hospital. Gardening, her friend and boss Abby Maitland McDermott had told her, was good therapy, a refreshing break from her high-pressure medical practice, but, Abby had added with a wink and a knowing nod, the right man might do Kate even more good than a horticultural hobby.

Once burned, twice shy, Kate had opted for the roses, thorns and all. She tugged on her gardening gloves, picked up the spade, and slammed it into the earth with the bottom of her heel. The resulting jolt almost knocked her backward.

Wiping sweat from her brow in Austin's late July heat, she positioned the gardening tool to try again. Visions of white roses climbing among the gingerbread columns and balustrades of the Victorian porch fueled her determination. This time she jumped on the spade with both feet, but the earth refused to give beneath her weight.

"Looks like you could use a hand—or at least a tougher foot."

She turned at the sound of the deep, drawling voice, and dreams of roses evaporated at the sight of the stunningly attractive man standing on her front walk with a huge black dog at his side.

He was a cowboy.

An honest-to-God cowboy.

Kate had been in Austin almost three years since moving from Atlanta, but in her obstetrical practice she'd treated only women. When she'd met her patients' husbands, they'd mostly been men who worked in offices downtown. In the sheltered grind of work and home, she had yet to come face-to-face with a legendary Texas cowpoke.

Until now.

Not only was the man who'd just spoken a cowboy, he was the most gorgeous specimen of masculine perfection she'd ever seen. Almost six feet tall, he had the lean, muscled look of someone who'd toted a few barges and lifted a few bales in his day. Broad, well-formed shoulders and impressive biceps filled his immaculately clean chambray shirt, rolled back at the cuffs to reveal powerful forearms. Tight jeans encased muscled thighs that could probably grip a horse with ease. A battered Stetson was clasped lightly in his right hand. His face was tanned, his brown hair sun-streaked, and his warm gray eyes the dusky color of a summer dawn. He emanated the confident aura of a man who knew where he wanted to go and how to get there. And who dared anyone to get in his way.

Striding toward her with the gait of someone more accustomed to horseback than sidewalks, he tossed his hat aside and took the spade from her. The huge black dog followed like a dark shadow.

"Looks like you've hit a tree root," the cowboy drawled. "You'll break your foot trying to dig it out in those flimsy shoes."

Suddenly aware of her own scruffy appearance, Kate glanced with dismay at her attire. Cutoff shorts, a faded sleeveless blouse tied at the waist, and raggedy tennis shoes, all perfect for working in the yard, but the worst possible apparel for meeting the most handsome man she'd ever seen. She pushed a strand of hair that had fallen free of her ponytail off her face—and felt the moist streak of dirt smeared on her cheek by her glove.

The cowboy, meanwhile, had set the spade over the spot where she'd been digging and jammed the sole of his well-worn boot against it. The blade sliced cleanly into the earth as if the ground were butter. With a practiced hand, he shifted to the other side of the spot and chopped the root there as well. With a few hefts of the spade, he removed roots and dirt from the hole.

"That oughta do it." The exertion hadn't left him the least bit winded, nor had he broken a sweat.

Flustered, Kate accepted the gardening tool he returned to her.

A wide smile softened the rough-hewn planes of his classically handsome face and revealed perfect teeth, gleaming white against his tan. "You don't talk much, do you?"

"I, uh, no. But thank you," Kate managed to stammer, still befuddled enough by the attractive stranger's sudden and unexpected assistance to have almost forgotten her manners.

"My pleasure, ma'am."

He even talks *like a cowboy,* Kate thought.

He pointed to the plant container she'd placed beside the hole. "Roses?"

She nodded toward the bush with its dark-green leaves and tight buds. She'd already deadheaded the spent blossoms. "Icebergs."

He arched his right eyebrow. "Interesting choice."

His comment was probably intended without innuendo, but it hit home nonetheless, and Kate made a conscious effort not to squirm. Other men had called her cold, but after what she'd suffered from Steven, she had earned the right to be downright chilly when it came to the opposite sex.

Besides, this man was too damned appealing, something she didn't want to deal with. Her life was just fine the way it was, without a handsome man stirring up her senses. She appreciated his help, but now she was ready to send him on his way.

"I like white roses," she said in defense of her Icebergs. "You have a better suggestion?" She doubted the cowboy knew anything about flowers and her challenge would be his cue to leave.

He moved back from the edge of the porch and studied the area. "I've had a lot of luck with Don

Juan ramblers myself. Plenty of blossoms, lots of deep red color, and like their famous namesake, they like the heat. They'd do well here.''

Kate stared at him. A cowboy who knew roses? And Don Juans, no less. Now *that* was an interesting choice. The thought of the infamous lover made her flush with unwanted images of the cowboy sweeping her off her feet, into his arms, and carrying her away. No, she really didn't need this distraction, but after he'd helped her, she couldn't be rude and simply tell him to move along.

''Or if you like pink,'' he said with a twinkle of mischief in his eyes as he glimpsed the color in her cheeks, ''you could plant Old Blush. They flourish in this part of the state.''

The fact that he'd noticed her face redden made her blush even more. What was the matter with her? Thirty-four years old, a full-fledged physician, and blushing like a schoolgirl.

''If you like,'' he was saying, ''I can plant this one for you.''

Clearing her mind of cowboy Don Juan images, Kate shook her head. ''I can't let you do that. After all, you were just passing by.''

''Well, ma'am, that's not exactly true.'' He pointed to the discreet sign by the front gate that advertised Shelley's Boardinghouse. ''You see, Bear—'' he jerked his thumb toward the dog that had stretched out in the shade of a nearby tree ''—and I are looking for a room.''

When he indicated the sign on the gate, she noticed

for the first time his truck parked on the street, a late-model pickup covered with the dust of long country miles.

"I'm Dean Harding," he said.

Resigned to enduring his too charming presence a few minutes longer, she tugged off her glove and offered him her hand. "Kate Purvis."

Her skin tingled at the feel of his warm, callused palm. As if she'd been burned, she dropped her hand, wanting to wipe away the seductive heat of his touch, but unwilling to reveal that the contact had affected her.

"I'm hoping to find work in Austin," Dean said.

"What kind of work?" Kate couldn't imagine anyone in the city needing a cowpoke, not even one with tantalizingly broad shoulders and a killer smile.

He shrugged. "Auto mechanic, carpentry. I'm good with my hands."

One glance at his long, capable fingers, and her imagination, fueled by references to Don Juan, ran wild again. With embarrassment, she felt her flush returning, and she mentally kicked herself. She was being ridiculous, going gaga over a total stranger. She found him entirely too intriguing and hated losing control of her reactions. The thought of him living under the same roof was disconcerting. The best plan was to send him on his way before she succumbed further to his charm.

"Too bad about the room," she said. "We're full up."

"Why, Kate Purvis!" Her mother's voice sounded from the porch behind her. "That's not true."

Kate glanced up to meet Dean Harding's questioning gaze full-on, but she couldn't tell if he was resentful or amused at her seeming deception. She hadn't lied. As far as she knew, all the rooms were rented.

With an inward groan, Kate turned and watched Shelley Purvis trundle through the screen door, a huge tray in her hands. Refreshments. Terrific. No quick exit for the cowboy now.

Dean Harding took the porch steps in one bound. "Let me help you with that, ma'am." He removed the loaded tray from Shelley's hands and placed it carefully on a wicker table on the broad front veranda.

"Saw you two working out here in this heat," Shelley said, "and figured you could use something cold to drink."

"That's mighty thoughtful, ma'am."

Thoughtful, my eye, Kate suspected. Her amiable mother was an incurable snoop who loved to know everything that went on around her. Knowing Shelley, she'd fixed the tray as an excuse to come out and get a look firsthand. In spite of her age, her mother hadn't lost her appreciation for a good-looking man. Kate suppressed a sigh. Dean Harding, it appeared, was as good-looking as they came.

The cowboy accepted a tall, frosty glass of what looked like her mother's famous peach tea. Kate had to give him credit. He'd barely blinked at her mother's appearance. A very young sixty, Shelley refused to yield to the indignities of growing older. A brilliant carrot color hid the gray in her hair. Despite her short, plump figure, she insisted on dressing like a teenager. Today she wore short overalls over an N'Sync T-shirt. Lace-up boots over socks with frilly lace cuffs completed her outfit—with the addition of a tiny press-on tattoo of a hummingbird on her right cheek. Kate sighed. The bird was an improvement. Yesterday had been a stiletto trailing drops of blood.

"Pardon my saying so, ma'am," Dean said to Shelley, "but you have magnificent hair. It's the color of a desert sunset."

Shelley preened at the compliment, and Kate glowered. The way the man was turning on the charm and her mother was lapping it up, she'd never get rid of him.

Resigned to the fact that the cowboy wasn't leaving as soon as she'd hoped, Kate climbed the steps, took a full glass from the tray, and plopped into the wicker swing at the opposite end of the porch. At least she no longer had to make conversation. Her mother, bless her, was the world's greatest talker.

"Thank you." Her mother glowed at the cowboy's compliment and handed him a napkin. "I'm Shelley Purvis, Kate's mother."

"You look more like her sister."

Kate groaned and slid deeper into the swing. Dean Harding had her mother eating out of his hand. As smitten as her mother seemed, she'd pitch him a tent in the backyard if she didn't have a room to rent him.

"I'm Dean Harding," the cowboy introduced himself to Shelley, "and that bundle of fur under the crape myrtle over there is Bear, my dog."

Shelley removed a deep bowl from the tray and set it on the porch floor. "I brought your dog some water."

At a signal from the cowboy, the dog climbed the porch steps, lapped water from the bowl, then sat beside the wicker rocker where Dean had settled.

Shelley passed him a plate of homemade cookies. He took one and hesitated. "Mind if Bear has one, too? She's awful partial to sweets."

"Take all you want. There's more in the kitchen," Shelley said. "Now, about that room—"

"I've already told Mr. Harding we're full," Kate called from her end of the porch. "Besides, Mother, you've always said you won't take pets."

"Now that's a real shame." Dean caught Kate's gaze and held it, gray eyes attempting to plumb the depths of her rejection, much to her discomfort. "This is exactly the kind of place we've been looking for. Right, Bear?"

The dog woofed softly in compliance.

Kate understood her need to send this handsome cowboy on his way, but of course her mother couldn't know how he disturbed her. He stirred her senses, something that hadn't happened since Steven walked out of her life over five years ago. After all that time, she was just beginning to regain her equilibrium. She didn't need a stranger around who made her remember what hormones were for.

"Not take pets? Don't be silly, Katie," her mother

said. "You know Felicity has her cats. And Bear here looks like a very well-behaved dog."

Bear was eating cookies from Dean's hand and licking any crumbs that fell to the porch floor.

Kate shook her head. "That doesn't change the fact we don't have a vacant room."

"Well, that's that, then." Dean set down his glass and rose to his feet. "Sorry to bother you, ladies. Thanks for the tea, Mrs.—"

"Purvis," her mother reminded him. "But you can call me Shelley. And sit back down. Kate doesn't know what she's talking about."

"Mother!"

This time, the cowboy didn't bother to hide his amusement. The corners of his generous mouth turned upward in a most appealing but infuriating way.

"Well, it's true," Shelley said to Kate. "You don't know, but it's not your fault. If you hadn't spent such long hours at the hospital yesterday—"

Dean's amusement disappeared, and he turned his remarkable gray eyes toward Kate. "Have you been sick?"

Shelley laughed. "Not my Katie. She's healthy as a horse. She's a doctor."

Dean settled his Stetson on his head, then pushed the brim off his forehead with his thumb. "Must be convenient to have a resident physician."

Kate snickered. "I don't think you'll be needing my services. I'm an OB-GYN."

"That's a moot point now, anyway." He gestured

to Bear and started down the steps. The dog followed at his heels.

"Wait," Shelley said. "Don't you want to hear about the room?"

Dean paused and turned, and his gaze locked with Kate's. "Guess I'm a mite confused. You have a room for rent or not?"

Kate shrugged. "Sounds like I'm out of the loop. Where did you conjure up another room, Mom?"

Shelley grinned, sending the hummingbird on her cheek into motion. "Felicity and I cleaned out that storage room on the second floor yesterday and put in a twin bed and some odds and ends. It's a bit small, Mr. Harding, and you'd have to share a bathroom with Raoul—"

"Raoul?" he said.

Kate slumped in the swing and sipped her tea. In spite of her best efforts, it looked as if the cowboy would be staying. She'd try not to notice. As busy as she stayed with her practice, maybe her overactive hormones wouldn't be a problem.

"Raoul Davega," Shelley was saying, "is a nice young man from South America. He's working as an air-conditioning repairman to earn enough money to move his family to the States."

"I don't mind sharing a bath," Dean said, "if Raoul doesn't."

"No problem," Shelley insisted. "I asked him yesterday when we were clearing out the storage room."

The screen door swung outward, and a small boy hurtled across the porch toward Bear. Terrified, Kate launched herself toward her son to intercept him before he reached the animal. Grim memories from her emergency-room days of a small child mauled by a dog speeded her movements.

"Mikey, no!" she screamed.

Mikey lunged straight for Bear. Kate rushed to grab him, but as she reached the dog, the cowboy snagged her around the waist and pulled her back against him.

"It's okay," he assured her with a calmness that soothed her frayed nerves. "Bear wouldn't harm a fly."

In spite of her panic, she noted that Dean smelled of leather and sunshine, and his body was hard and firm. A *good* feeling, she realized with a jolt, and suffered a twinge of disappointment when he released her. She could still feel the imprint of his arm around her waist, gauge the warmth of his breath against her neck, see the heat in his eyes.

She noted that for the first time since his arrival, the cowboy looked distracted, and she groaned inwardly again. If he was feeling what *she* was feeling, she was in big trouble.

By now Mikey had his arms around Bear's neck, his face buried in her fur. Bear sat unmoving, docilely accepting the boy's affection.

Dean dragged his simmering gaze from Kate and spoke to Mikey. "Her name's Bear."

"Cool! Is she a *real* bear?"

Dean shook his head. "I call her Bear because she looks like one. She's a black Labrador."

Mikey cocked his head in the way that always tugged at Kate's heart. "What's a labrador?"

"A black lab's a dog. Do you have a dog?"

Mikey shook his head. "I'm only five. Mommy says I hafta wait till I'm bigger."

Dean smiled. "You look pretty big already."

Kate shot the cowboy an annoyed look. She didn't need this man in her life, and Mikey definitely didn't need a dog.

Mikey raised his face toward Kate, his wide brown eyes a mirror image of her own. "I like her, Mommy. Can I keep her?"

Kate shook her head. "She's Mr. Harding's dog."

"But you can play with her whenever you like." Dean raised his gaze to Kate's. In the late-afternoon light, the gray in his eyes had turned to silver. "That is, if it's all right with your mother."

Kind of Dean Harding to consult her, she thought with uncharacteristic sarcasm, but she couldn't resist Mikey, who could wrap her around his little finger. "Why don't you find an old tennis ball? Maybe Bear would like to play catch."

"Okay." The boy turned to the dog with a solemn expression. "Don't go away, Bear. I'll be right back." He raced into the house, slamming the screen door behind him. Kate could hear his tennis shoes thundering up the stairs.

Shelley stood. "I have to help Felicity with dinner. Do you want that room, Mr. Harding? Meals are included." She quoted him a rate.

"Sounds reasonable," the cowboy said. "I'll try it

for a week and see how it suits Bear and me, if that's okay with you.''

"We're happy to have you,'' Shelley said. "Kate, you sit here while Mr. Harding finishes his tea, then show him his room.'' She turned to Dean with a smile that made the hummingbird flutter on her cheek. "Hope you like fried chicken and potato salad. That's our menu for tonight.''

"Home cooking will be a real treat.'' With a satisfied grin, Dean settled back into the wicker rocker, and Bear lay at his feet.

Kate had no choice but to sit across from the man she'd had no success in getting rid of. She could always hope that the tiny room wouldn't suit him, but she doubted that. He seemed about the most agreeable person she'd ever met.

Then why are you so anxious for him to leave? an inner voice tweaked her.

Because he reminds me I'm a woman. Life was a lot more comfortable when I'd forgotten.

Good thing you remembered, the inner voice responded. *Comfortable can be damned dull.*

"He's a fine boy,'' Dean was saying.

Kate abandoned her inner debate. "Mikey? He's all boy. He keeps us on our toes around here.''

As if on cue, Mikey burst through the front door, tennis ball in hand. "C'mon, Bear. Let's play!''

The dog didn't move until Dean spoke. "It's okay, Bear. Go on.''

"Stay inside the fence,'' Kate warned.

"Bear will see to it,'' Dean assured her.

"She can do that?"

"She used to watch the cook's children on the ranch."

"You worked on a ranch?" Immediately Kate wanted to smack herself for her dumb question. Where else would a cowboy work? What was the matter with her brain?

"Off and on." Dean kept his eyes on the dog and the boy, as if avoiding her gaze.

He obviously wasn't going to discuss that aspect of his past, so she took another tack, knowing her mother would grill her later for details. "Are you from around here?"

"San Antonio."

With such succinct answers, he wasn't telling her much. Giving up her interrogation, she pushed to her feet. "Want to see the room?"

"Sure." He whistled to the dog. "Bear, keep an eye on Mikey."

Kate motioned for him to precede her inside, but he insisted on holding the door for her, a display of old-fashioned manners she found strangely appealing. Climbing the stairs to the rooms on the second floor, she was all too aware of him behind her and wished again she wasn't wearing tight, faded cutoffs. She sighed. Why should she care what he thought of her?

Because he's the most intriguing man you've met in over five years.

Hoping to silence the provocative voice in her head, she hurried down the second-floor hall to a small room at the end and flung open the door.

Her mouth gaped in surprise. Her mother had worked a miracle. What had once been a cramped, dusty storeroom was now an attractive bedroom. A twin bed stood against one wall, a table and chair beneath the double windows, and a recliner in the corner.

Recovering from her astonishment, she stepped aside for Dean to enter. "All the comforts of home."

He went immediately to the bed, sat and bounced up and down. Glancing up, he smiled. "Perfect. I'll take it."

Seeing the handsome cowboy on the bed set off her imagination again, which, fueled by hormones, assaulted her with visions of a strong, bare body, twisted sheets and hot kisses. She felt a flush working its way up her neck to her face. Before she made an utter fool of herself, she swiveled on her heel and fled the room.

"Dinner in thirty minutes," she called over her shoulder.

WITH BEAR CURLED under the table at his feet, Dean Harding surveyed the spacious dining room of Shelley Purvis's boardinghouse and stifled his discomfort. He was used to eating alone. And having all these people around was going to make his job a whole lot harder.

Shelley Purvis sat at the head of the huge mahogany table and passed bowls heaped with potato salad and platters filled with sliced melons and fried chicken. One thing for sure, he wouldn't go hungry while he was here. He sighed, reluctantly considering good cooking an almost fair trade for his lack of solitude. He wouldn't want for conversation at the Purvis table. Shelley kept up a lively chatter throughout the meal, drawing each person into the exchange.

Except her daughter Kate.

Kate and her son Mikey sat across the table from Dean. And Kate had barely spoken a word since the meal began. She looked different from the way she had in the yard, more like a typical know-it-all doctor in her tailored blouse and skirt. She'd abandoned the casual ponytail with escaping curls. Tonight her thick brown hair, the kind a man would like to run his fingers through, hung to her shoulders. He decided he'd liked her better when she was trying to plant that rose. She'd seemed such a pretty little thing with her long bare legs and slim tanned arms, and not a fraction over five foot four. The top of her head had barely reached his nose. In spite of the heat, she'd smelled of lilacs—

Dean brought himself up short. What was he thinking? Kate Purvis was a doctor, a member of that arrogant, often incompetent profession that had wreaked havoc in his life. He'd like the woman a whole lot more if she were a housewife and a gardener, adorable in shorts and tennis shoes with a smear of dirt across her cheek. He'd had his fill of doctors, enough to last two lifetimes.

Glancing at her little boy chewing on a chicken leg, Dean wondered about Mikey's father. Kate had apparently retained her maiden name, although some women did that for professional reasons, but he'd seen no sign at the boardinghouse of anyone who might be Mikey's dad.

"Mr. Harding," Shelley said, "let me introduce you to everyone." She nodded toward the tall, thin, white-haired woman at the other end of the table. "This is my friend and fellow chef, Felicity Trent. We've been friends since we were children growing up together in Atlanta. She moved here with us to help run the boardinghouse."

"I hope the meal meets with your approval," Felicity said with a friendly welcome in her blue eyes.

"Delicious," Dean said. "I haven't had such a good meal since before my mother died."

He'd obviously struck the right chord, because Felicity beamed with pleasure and blushed like a girl. Kate, however, frowned, and he wondered why, until he reminded himself the woman hadn't exactly taken to him from the start. He was going to have to work harder at gaining her acceptance. He would eventually need her cooperation.

"You've met Kate and Mikey," Shelley continued, then gestured to the young woman on her left. "And this is Naomi Reddy, our resident actress."

Naomi must be nervous or ill, or watching her weight, for she'd only picked at her food. A tall, striking woman with golden hair, too much makeup, and oversize dangling earrings, she acknowledged Dean with a regal nod that set her jewelry bobbing. "You'll have to come to the opening of our play day after tomorrow."

"Which play?" he asked.

"We're doing *My Fair Lady* at the dinner theater. I'm playing Eliza Doolittle."

Mikey looked up from his chicken leg. "Yeah, she can sing so loud the windows rattle."

"Mikey," Kate muttered beside him, her face turning the becoming pink Dean had noted earlier.

"Well, she can," the boy insisted. "Just ask Nana."

Shelley busied herself passing another platter of chicken and pretended not to hear her grandson.

Naomi shot the boy a wilting look. "In the theater, we call it projecting."

"And next to you, Dean," Shelley continued before Mikey could say more, "is Raoul."

Dean nodded to the swarthy man who looked to be in his late twenties. "We met in the hall upstairs. Guess Raoul, Mikey and I are the only men around here."

"You can never have too many pretty women," Raoul remarked with latino gallantry.

Dean was watching Kate, wondering if she'd speak up about the absence of other men. Maybe she had a husband who was late for dinner. As if to avoid Dean, she kept her attention fixed on her plate.

"No, you're not the only males," Shelley informed him. "There's Peter Tirrell."

"You won't see much of him," Kate said, but her tone was neutral.

"Does he work nights?" Dean asked.

"No," Shelley explained, "he's just very shy. He's

a computer troubleshooter for the phone company. Takes all his meals in his rooms.''

"He's creepy," Mikey volunteered.

"Mikey!" Kate's voice shot up an octave, and her color deepened. "That's not nice."

"Sorry, Mommy," he mumbled. "But he sneaks around all the time."

"Like Nana said," Kate explained, "Mr. Tirrell is shy. He's uncomfortable around people."

Dean accepted a bowl of peach cobbler topped with vanilla ice cream and did some mental arithmetic. Seven other people lived in the house. Naomi would be out late with her show, Peter stayed in his room, Mikey probably went to bed early, and, with any luck, Kate would have rounds at the hospital. That left only Shelley, Felicity and Raoul to avoid. Obviously, some evening after dark would be the best time to accomplish the work he had to do.

Quiet descended on the table while dessert was consumed, but the peacefulness was soon broken by Shelley. "Kate, how about showing Mr. Harding the rest of the house?"

Kate glanced up from her plate with a look like a wild animal startled by bright lights. "I have rounds—"

"You'll have time," Shelley assured her.

Dean smothered a grin. He'd run into matchmaking mamas before, so Shelley Purvis was wasting her time on him. If there was one woman Dean definitely wasn't interested in, it was a female doctor. But he couldn't be rude. He needed to stay on everyone's good side to accomplish his goal.

"I'd love to see the house, Ms. Purvis," he said to Kate. "Better learn my way around so I don't bust in where I'm not supposed to."

Lips set in resignation, Kate stood. "Finish your dessert, Mikey, then help Nana and Felicity clear the table. Mr. Harding, if you'll come with me?"

She went into the wide hallway that served as a foyer, and Dean followed, trailed by Bear.

"Call me Dean," he said.

"If you like." She walked across the hallway into the room opposite the dining room, and he had to admit, when he wasn't thinking of her as a doctor, she had a damned appealing shape that filled out her tailored skirt and blouse in all the right places. Then he realized she hadn't responded with permission to use *her* first name. Just when he'd thought she might warm up to him, she'd given him the cold shoulder.

"This is the parlor." At her voice, his attention snapped back to his surroundings. "It's open to all our guests. There's a television, a telephone for local calls, and you can usually find the day's newspaper here."

"Must get kinda crowded when you bring home a date," he observed, "what with all these boarders filling up the front room."

"My dates are none of your business," she snapped.

"Just a friendly observation," he drawled. "No need to be defensive."

He wondered if her touchiness meant she didn't date or simply that she didn't bring her dates home. Pink tinged her cheeks, and she looked less like a doctor and more like a woman. A hell of a handsome woman. She brushed past him as she headed back into the hall, and the scent of lilacs filled his nostrils, reminding him of hot summer nights and slow kisses.

She walked down the hall and turned left. He followed her into a gigantic kitchen with tall windows that let in lots of sunshine, a pleasant room with delectable aromas that brought back memories of his mother's kitchen. Bear's sniffer was going a mile a minute.

"Guests are free to use the kitchen at all hours." Kate was strictly business.

She hadn't met his eyes since she'd snapped at him, and he wondered if he'd unconsciously telegraphed his dislike of doctors. Something about him was making her very uncomfortable. If he didn't know better, he could almost believe she knew the real reason he'd rented a room in her house.

"Mother leaves snacks in the fridge on the lower shelf, and if you want to keep a stock of your favorite cold drinks, there's plenty of room. Just beware of Naomi."

"Why?"

"She considers anything in the fridge fair game. She drank all Mikey's fruit punch one night."

"From what I saw at dinner, she doesn't eat much."

"Not before a performance," Kate said. "But after a show she gets a bad case of the munchies."

"Is it okay if I feed Bear in here?"

Apparently warming up to Dean, Kate leaned down and scratched Bear behind the ears. "Sure. But if you want her on a strict diet, watch out for Mother and Felicity. They'll sneak her tidbits. Sometimes I think they see fattening up everyone in the house as their sole mission in life."

He regarded her trim figure appraisingly. "You seem to have resisted just fine."

Going cold again at his compliment, Kate hurried back into the hall and stood before a closed door. "This is my home office. It's off-limits to everyone. The room behind my study is Felicity's. She likes being close to the kitchen."

Dean swore to himself. Kate's study, the one room he needed access to, was right next to Felicity Trent's. He hoped the older woman wasn't a light sleeper.

"All the other boarders' rooms are on the second floor," Kate said, "and the family's rooms are on the third floor."

"I get the picture." He flashed her his broadest smile. "You make a great tour guide. Thanks for showing me around."

She continued to avoid his gaze. "If you'll excuse me—"

She turned to leave, but he caught her by the wrist. Her skin was warm and soft, and he had to resist the impulse to rub circles on its satiny surface with his thumb. "Have I offended you somehow?"

Her head jerked up, and for the second time that evening, her eyes met his. She had that deer-in-the-headlights look again, all flustered and ill at ease. "I'm sorry, I'm just very busy...."

"Seems to me it's more than that," he said reasonably.

"More than what?"

"Busy. I get the feeling you don't like me."

"That's not true. I just..." Her voice trailed off. She stood only inches away, her head tilted up to meet his gaze, her lilac fragrance teasing his senses, her lips pink and moist. For an instant, he found himself wanting to kiss her—before common sense kicked in and reminded him where he was and why.

Reluctantly, he released her wrist. "Thanks again for the tour. I won't keep you any longer."

She turned and fled, just as she had from his room earlier, and he heard her footsteps rapidly ascending the stairs.

He followed more slowly, and when he reached his room on the second floor, she had already disappeared.

Smiling, he scratched his chin. The woman was a fascinating puzzle, running hot one minute and cold the next. He shook his head. *She* wasn't the puzzle he was here to solve.

Removing Bear's food and dishes from his bag, he returned to the kitchen, fed the dog and filled her bowl with water. Then, with patience wrought of long practice, he reentered his room and pulled a book from his duffel bag. Bear turned around three times and nestled on the hand-braided rug beside the bed.

Before Dean settled in the recliner to read, he dug deeper into his bag, extracted his kit of lock-picking tools and slid them beneath the mattress.

In a few days, he'd be needing them.

CHAPTER TWO

HUMMING A HAPPY TUNE beneath her breath, Kate shoved her tray down the line of the hospital cafeteria and selected a tossed salad and iced tea. In spite of problems she'd encountered at work that morning, she was having a fine day.

It had started when she'd awakened at five o'clock with a smile on her lips and a lightness in her heart she hadn't experienced in years. Since Steven's desertion, she'd been numb toward other men, impervious to their charms. Now with Dean Harding's appearance, she felt as if a part of her that was dead had suddenly come to life again.

She'd had a hard time getting to sleep the night before. All she could do was toss and turn, thinking of the handsome stranger asleep in the room below hers. When he'd first appeared, she'd been reluctant to deal with her own reactions and had wanted him gone. But the longer she lay awake, the more she realized she was still a young, healthy woman in the prime of her life, at her sexual peak. Maybe a little masculine attention was just what she needed. She'd learned a lot about herself from her disastrous affair with Steven. She could handle a harmless flirtation and keep it within reasonable bounds.

Dean Harding had thrown her off balance, catching her by surprise. Tomorrow, she promised herself as she waited for sleep, she'd take control of herself, her feelings and her reactions. And she'd enjoy the cowboy's company instead of running away from it.

Finally at peace with herself and her decision, she'd drifted off and slept soundly until her alarm roused her.

She had dressed quickly and crept quietly downstairs, not wanting to awaken the others. When she reached the first floor, the aroma of coffee brewing announced that someone had risen ahead of her. She guessed Felicity was having another bout of insomnia, but when she entered the kitchen, Dean sat at the kitchen table, his strong, lean fingers curled around a large mug.

She wouldn't have thought it possible, but he looked even more attractive than he had the day before. Freshly shaven cheeks accentuated the strong lines of his jaw, and in spite of the early hour, his gray eyes were bright and clear. Thick, brown hair, shot with sun streaks and neatly combed, matched the plaid of his shirt. Behind him, Bear crunched happily on a bowl of dry food in the corner by the back door. Her tail wagged in welcome at Kate's entrance.

With flawless manners, Dean rose to his feet. "Good morning."

"Morning." She went to the cupboard for a mug and filled it with coffee, glad for an activity to hide her too obvious pleasure at their predawn meeting. "You're up early."

"Force of habit, left over from my days as a ranch hand." His deep voice resonated pleasantly in her ears, and she had a fleeting notion of what it might be like to awaken to such a voice and such a face every morning.

She sipped the coffee, hot and black, the way she liked it. "It's nice to have coffee already made."

"What gets you up before dawn?" He circled the table and pulled out the chair across from his for her.

"Morning rounds." She sat, and he returned to his chair. "I'm up at five seven days a week."

His congenial smile brightened the dim room and flooded her with a pleasurable warmth. "What's it like, being a doctor?"

She took another taste of the strong, hot brew. "I love bringing babies into the world and seeing the happiness on their parents' faces."

"Must be a pretty heady feeling, all that power of life and death over folks."

For a few seconds, she thought his eyes hardened and his mouth tightened, but a trick of the overhead fluorescent lights must have created the illusion, because the next instant his expression was as warm and pleasing as before. The man was an intriguing paradox of gentleness and strength.

"It's not a question of power," she insisted. "Being a doctor is about helping people. That's what I love about my work."

"Liking what you do makes up for the long hours?"

She was flattered that he'd taken an interest. "Almost. I often wish I had more free time."

"You have rounds every evening, too?"

"Unless I can get someone to cover for me so I can have time to spend with Mikey."

"Working late tonight?"

"Probably. Often I don't know until the last minute."

She'd finished her coffee and left, but now she wondered why he'd asked about this evening. Surely he hadn't planned on asking her for a date.

And would that be so awful? her inner voice demanded.

Happiness bubbled up inside her. No, a date with Dean Harding wouldn't be awful at all. In fact, she was quite taken with the concept.

She paid the cafeteria cashier and glimpsed Abby Maitland McDermott, chief OB-GYN at the hospital, seated at a nearby table. Abby caught her eye and motioned for Kate to join her. Kate worked her way through the noonday crowd and sat beside her boss and friend. She and Abby had met in medical school and became close friends. Abby's offer of a position at Maitland Maternity had brought Kate and her family to Austin.

"Busy morning?" Abby asked.

Kate nodded. "A breech birth and a case of septicemia."

"Everyone okay?"

"Mother and daughter are fine. And I've started IVs of antibiotics, glucose and saline on the septic patient. I think we've averted shock, but we're monitoring her closely.''

Abby shoved a lock of brown hair behind her ear. The hospital chief physician was only a year younger than Kate, and her girlish looks belied her professional competency, but Abby ran a tight ship, and Kate had the utmost respect for her as a doctor as well as affection for her as a friend.

''That explains it,'' Abby said.

Kate swallowed a bite of salad. ''What explains what?''

''You must be pleased with your success. You're glowing today.'' Abby's lips lifted in an impish grin, and her dark eyes sparkled. ''If I didn't know better, I'd say you were pregnant.''

Kate choked on a lettuce leaf and coughed to clear her throat. ''Pregnant! You've got to be kidding. As I recall from my med school days, it takes a man to get a woman in the family way. How many men do you see around me?''

Abby giggled. ''Well, there's Dr. Winslow over by the window.''

Kate smacked her friend on the arm. ''Get real. He's over sixty-five and has been married to the same woman for almost forty years.''

Abby tilted her head and studied Kate with a penetrating gaze. ''There's a man in your life, isn't there?''

Remembering the handsome cowboy who'd walked into her yard the previous day and shared coffee with her that morning, Kate lowered her gaze and cut her tomato wedge with surgical precision. "Why would you think that?"

"Like I said, you're glowing. Must be hormones—unless you're running a fever." Abby's voice ended on an upward note, like a question.

But it was a question Kate refused to answer. She was still unsure exactly how she felt about the attractive man who had made her feel like a woman again for the first time since Mikey was born.

"Tell you what," she promised her friend. "If there ever is a man in my life, you'll be the first to know."

Abby grinned. "The first to know after Shelley, you mean. You can never hide anything from that mother of yours."

Kate laughed. "You're right about that. Sometimes I think she has a spy satellite contract with the CIA. Nothing else explains how she ferrets out her information."

Abby's expression sobered and she placed her hand over Kate's. "Just be careful in the male department, won't you? You've been hurt before. I don't want to see you hurt again."

"Don't be silly," Kate insisted. "Just because Steven and my father are cads doesn't mean all men are rotten."

Later, as she made her afternoon rounds, Kate remembered that declaration with a smile. She had a good feeling about Dean Harding. She was willing to bet he'd turn out to be a winner.

And if anyone was due for a winner, she was.

INHERENTLY A LONER who preferred his own company, Dean found himself surprisingly at ease with the other men in the room. He had the greatest respect for William Garrett and his son Dylan, and Mitch Barnes, a former FBI agent. Perhaps the common bond he had with both ranchers and lawmen created the atmosphere of easy camaraderie.

Or maybe his comfort was due to the liberal amount of smooth Kentucky bourbon over ice in the glass at his elbow. Or the luxurious depth of the leather chair that fit his backside better than his own saddle. Or maybe he was just softening with age. After all, he'd be thirty-six next month.

Or maybe it was the memory of a pretty little woman with big brown eyes and silky brown hair that had made him so mellow. He'd had a hard time getting Kate Purvis out of his mind since first meeting her yesterday.

Even if she was a doctor.

Whatever the reason for his relaxation, he was enjoying himself. He leaned down to Bear, curled at his feet, and scratched her behind the ears. The dog, his constant companion for the past six years, lifted her head and scanned the room with watchful, dark eyes. Apparently sensing no danger, she promptly fell asleep once more.

"Any luck yet, Dean?" William Garrett, the patriarch of the Double G Ranch outside San Antonio in whose great room they were meeting, stood at the massive stone fireplace. The athletic-looking sixty-one-year-old propped a booted foot on the hearth, cold now in the July heat and filled with lacy summer ferns. Leaning an elbow on the mantel, he fastened ocean-blue eyes on his visitor.

"I've found evidence of a birth in Austin that could be what we're looking for," Dean admitted, "but I've hit the wall of doctor-patient privilege. These blasted doctors are tighter than a miser's fist with information about their patients."

"Double damn!" Opposite Dean, Mitch Barnes pounded the arm of his chair in frustration. "We'll never find Terry at this rate."

Dean observed Mitch with sympathy. Last spring, while recuperating from an injury to his Achilles tendon, Mitch had discovered he was the father of an infant daughter, left at the apartment building where he was staying. The baby's mother, Terry Monteverde, had disappeared and, at first, was assumed to have drowned. A subsequent investigation found that Terry was still alive but running for her life from a diamond smuggler, Leo Hayes, who had tried to incriminate her with his schemes.

"I have a plan," Dean explained. "By posing as a health insurance rep, I learned Kate Purvis was the doctor on duty the night the baby with matching stats was born. Since Kate's office wouldn't deal with my questions by phone, I'm doing some snooping on my own. I've taken a room in her mother's boardinghouse where Kate also lives. As soon as it's safe, probably one night this week, I'll search her home office, see if she keeps any records of births there."

"Is this cloak-and-dagger routine our only option?'' Dylan Garrett asked. Dylan, along with his twin sister Lily, was founder of Finders Keepers, a detective agency that specialized in locating missing persons, and he'd hired Dean to track down Terry through local birth records. The agency's office was at the Double G Ranch, where Dylan lived with Lily's family and his father William. The youngest sibling, Ashley, lived in downtown San Antonio. ''With unauthorized searches, you could be treading on the margins of the law.''

Dean shrugged. ''We may have to bend a few rules to find Terry Monteverde, especially since she doesn't want to be found.''

William tapped his chin with his index finger. ''I doubt Terry knows that Leo Hayes is dead and no longer a threat to her.''

With his keen lawman's eye, Dean observed with a start that the two younger men flanking William on either side of the fireplace looked enough alike to be brothers. Though Dylan's hair was light brown and Mitch's dark, both men were over six feet tall and had the same keen blue eyes. Dean shoved the strange notion aside as Dylan directed another question his way.

''What's your next move?'' he asked.

Dean swirled the ice in his bourbon, then took a swallow. The smooth whiskey slid down his throat and warmed his insides as he formulated an answer. ''Like I said, I wait until it's safe to search the doctor's records. If the baby was Hope, maybe Kate's records will have an address for Terry.''

"How long before you can search?" Mitch asked with growing impatience. "Hope needs her mother."

"That's true," William agreed, "but you're doing a damned good job as a single dad, Mitch."

Mitch grinned at William. "I've been lucky to have you and Lily to turn to for advice."

Dean knew that Mitch had grown close to William over the last couple of months. Both William and his older daughter, Lily, a new mother herself, had been generous in sharing their time and experience with Mitch. In fact, William's interest in Mitch and Hope's situation had prompted Dylan to ask his father's help and counsel on their case.

"Now," William said, not bothering to hide his pleasure at Mitch's praise, "if you fellows will excuse me, I have a ranch to run."

When William left the room, Dean drained his glass and stood. "I'd better head back to Austin."

Mitch and Dylan walked to the door with him. "Who's looking after your ranch while you're gone?" Dylan asked.

"My neighbor Luis Jimenez and his son Jorge. They've filled in for me before when I've worked other cases for you."

"You miss police work?" Mitch asked.

Dean recalled his years on the force in San Antonio, the experience that had caused Dylan to seek Dean's help on previous cases, and shook his head. "I don't miss witnessing the worst in folks day in and day out one bit. I enjoy the peace and quiet of the ranch. Besides, the cases Dylan assigns me are just enough to keep my investigative skills sharp. What about you? You going back to work at the Bureau once your Achilles tendon is healed?''

Mitch shook his head. ''I resigned for good. I've grown fond of this part of Texas, so I've applied for a deputy position with the sheriff's office. I should hear soon.''

''You're an experienced lawman. They'd be fools not to take you.''

Mitch grinned. ''I'm counting on them thinking that.'' Then his expression turned anxious. ''You think you'll turn up something on Terry soon?''

''As soon as I can.'' Dean grasped Mitch's shoulder. ''Trust me. I'll find her for you, friend. I know too well what it's like to lose the woman you love.''

Dean said goodbye to the two men and headed out the door, Bear trotting beside him. If he hurried, he could be back in Austin in plenty of time for supper.

HALFWAY THROUGH her afternoon shift, Kate suddenly remembered the rosebush she'd been planting the previous afternoon. With the unexpected arrival of Dean Harding, she had completely forgotten the plant, and she thought of it lying now where she'd left it, beside the hole the accommodating cowboy had dug. Chagrined at being such a scatterbrain, she vowed to plant the blasted thing as soon as she finished work.

Returning from the hospital later that afternoon, she found Dean in the front yard, watering the newly planted rosebush at the base of the front porch.

The thumb of one hand tucked in the front pocket of his jeans and the sleeves of his shirt rolled almost to his elbows, he brandished the garden hose with his other hand, emanating as much rugged appeal as if he'd been roping cattle instead of irrigating flowers. With a happy woof, Bear lumbered up to greet her.

"You shouldn't have done that." Embarrassment gave a sharp edge to her voice.

He raised one eyebrow and the corners of his mouth quirked as if he were suppressing a grin. "I can dig it back up if you like. Put it back in that pot where you left it."

To hide her humiliation, she ducked her head and scratched Bear behind the ears. "Of course not."

"I interrupted you yesterday," he said with a warmth in his voice that threatened to turn her bones to butter. "Planting your rosebush was the least I could do."

"Thanks." What kind of idiot did he think she was, totally forgetting a job she'd started? "You've saved me one chore tonight before I go back to the hospital."

He seemed taller in the afternoon sun. The light glinted off his face and arms, turning his tanned skin to gold. With a powerful flick of his wrist, he shut off the faucet and rewound the hose.

"You're not going back to the hospital," he called over his shoulder.

"I'm not?" She wondered if this was his way of asking her out. If so, she wasn't sure she liked a man making decisions for her. He'd already presumed too much, planting her rosebush.

Drying his hands on his jeans, he approached her. "Your mama's made other plans."

"Oh."

"We're going on a picnic at Zilker Park."

"We are?" Now she was thoroughly confused.

Sitting on the porch steps, he stretched his long legs in front of him and reclined on his elbows. Bear sat beside him. "Raoul and Peter are working late. Naomi has an early dress rehearsal. Felicity is at her African Violet Society's monthly dinner. So your mama decided the rest of us should take a picnic supper to the park."

"But she knows I have evening rounds."

He nodded. "She called your boss, uh—"

"Abby?"

"That's right. Asked Abby to find someone to cover for you."

Kate plopped down on the stairs beside him in surprise. "Why would Mother do that?"

He cocked his head in a way that reminded her of Mikey. "She told me you're working too hard."

"But—"

"Don't look a gift horse in the mouth," he said in his slow, soft way that played pleasantly on her senses. "Just take advantage of your night off. From what you told me this morning, you don't get many."

"Mommy!" The screen door slammed behind her, and Mikey jumped on her back, his arms around her neck. "Nana says we're going on a picnic!"

Kate hugged and kissed her son, then raised an eyebrow at Dean. "Why am I always the last one to know what's going on around here?"

He fixed her with an intense look that darkened his gray eyes to charcoal. "Maybe your mama's right. You spend too much time working."

She turned away, unable to meet his gaze. The man had depths she couldn't fathom. "I'm a doctor. My patients need me."

Mikey tightened his arms around her. "I need you, too, Mommy."

Conscience pricked her. In spite of all her best intentions, she never spent as much time with Mikey as she wanted. She enveloped her son in another fierce hug. "I love you, tiger."

Mikey quickly wriggled free. "Can we go now?"

She rose to her feet. "We have to change first. Come with me and we'll find your swim trunks."

Kate left Dean lounging on the front steps with an inscrutable expression that could have been anything from boredom to cunning. She had always relied on hard work and perseverance, because she didn't believe in blind luck. But if it wasn't due to good fortune, why had a cowboy handsome enough for Hollywood central casting and with irresistible charm suddenly shown up on her doorstep?

And what did he really want?

THREE HOURS LATER, lounging on the blanket where they'd spread their picnic, sated from her mother's delicious meal, Kate still hadn't figured out her cowboy. His manners were impeccable, his charm seductive, his attention to Mikey admirable. But why was he spending time with them when he could have been hitting the night spots of Austin like so many other single men his age?

While Kate and her mother had unpacked the picnic supper, Dean had taught Mikey to play catch, as patiently as if the boy had been his own. Praising Mikey each time he caught the ball and encouraging him even when he missed it, Dean had made the exercise fun as well as instructive. He and Mikey had laughed together as Bear chased the balls Mikey missed, and Kate could see that Dean's easy acceptance of her son's limited ability made Mikey try even harder to please the cowboy.

During supper, Dean had included Mikey in the conversation instead of ignoring him as many adults would have done, and Mikey had surprised even her with his repertoire of knock-knock jokes. Dean brought out the best in Mikey, and Kate lamented anew that her son had no permanent male role model in his life. But kind and encouraging as Dean was, did she really want her son modeling his behavior after a cowboy drifter?

Shelley, looking like a teenager in shocking-pink Bermuda shorts with a boat-neck top in matching pink-and-orange stripes, had just led Mikey away toward Barton Springs and a short swim before heading home. Kate's gaze followed the pair through the masses of people in the park, guided by her mother's pink tennis shoes and pink straw hat.

"She's a remarkable woman," Dean said.

"You don't know the half of it."

"Tell me."

Kate eyed him skeptically, but he seemed genuinely interested in her mother. "She was married to my father for thirty years, the perfect doctor's wife—"

"Your dad was a doctor, too?" His expression changed slightly, as if in distaste, then the angle of light through the trees shifted somewhat, and Dean's face seemed as interested and congenial as before.

"He still is. A plastic surgeon."

"So a love of medicine runs in the family?"

"Not really. My father is more interested in money than his patients. And he made tons of it."

"Sounds like a lot of doctors I know."

This time there was no mistaking the bitterness in his voice, and she wondered whether tragedy or simple prejudice had put it there. "We're not all like that. In it for the money, I mean. Most of us aren't."

He said nothing.

"Four years ago my father decided money wasn't enough. He wanted a beautiful young wife to go with it. He divorced my mother."

"Sounds like she was lucky to be rid of him."

Kate shook her head. "She didn't think so at the time. Her whole life had revolved around my father, being the perfect hostess, heading the hospital auxiliary. You wouldn't know it to look at her now, but I never saw my mother in anything but a tasteful dress or suit while I was growing up. She was very conscious of her image as a doctor's wife.''

Dean grinned. ''Looks like she's busted loose from those ropes.''

His bitterness had disappeared, and Kate liked him better this way. She smiled back. ''After Dad left, she pulled herself together, decided to be her own person. With her divorce settlement, she bought the house in Austin. When I took the job at Maitland Maternity we moved here from Atlanta. She's been happy as a lark ever since.''

''Do you still see your father?''

The emptiness she'd felt since the divorce yawned inside her. ''Occasionally.''

Dean shook his head. ''Mikey's a great kid. If he were my grandchild, I couldn't get enough of him.''

''My father's priorities have shifted since he married Jennifer. And he's always been embarrassed by the circumstances of Mikey's—'' Dean's open manner had lured her into revealing more than she'd intended to a man who was almost a stranger.

''Circumstances?''

She took a deep breath and plunged ahead to finish what she'd started. He might as well know. ''Mikey's father and I were never married.''

Dean said nothing, and for some strange reason, she felt compelled to explain. ''Steven, Mikey's father, was a resident in the same hospital with me. We were crazy in love and planned to be married. When I became pregnant, Steven started making excuses to delay the wedding. The month before Mikey was born, Steven dumped me for an airheaded nurse who worked in the ER. I was devastated. My mom, bless her, said it was better I found out about Steven's lack of commitment *before* I married him. She tried to console me by saying at least I'd been spared a messy divorce.''

''And your father?''

''The fact that I was an unwed mother was a great humiliation to him.''

''Pardon my saying so, but from what you've told me about your dad, sounds like your mama—and you and Mikey—are better off without him.''

Kate nodded as Shelley's pink straw hat disappeared from sight. ''Mother came to that conclusion herself a couple years ago. It's been very liberating for her.''

Dean reached for a fresh peach from the basket beside him and offered her one. When she declined, he took a bite of the fruit and sweet juice ran down his chin. She handed him a napkin, and as he took it, their knuckles grazed. The warmth of his skin sent a jolt of pleasure through her.

Flustered, she searched for a topic to fill the charged silence. ''You went job hunting today?''

''Uh-huh.''

''Any luck?''

''Nope.''

''And you accused me of not talking much.''

''I did?''

''Yesterday, when you first came to the house.''

He finished the peach, wiped his hands on the napkin and shoved to his feet. "I'm real talkative when there's something to say, but nothing worked out today."

She cocked her head, an unconscious imitation of her son's favorite gesture, and studied him. Something in his statement didn't ring true, and she couldn't tell if he was hiding something or simply awkward with the direction of the conversation. Some men felt being out of work reflected negatively on their masculinity. Maybe Dean Harding was one of them, and dwelling on it embarrassed him.

He reached into a mesh bag Shelley had packed with the picnic and pulled out a neon-yellow Frisbee. "Want to play?"

She couldn't tell if the heat in his eyes was intentional or caused by the slanting rays of the setting sun. Things were moving too fast for her. Only once before had she been so immediately attracted to a man. Mikey was the result.

And in addition to that overwhelming joy had been a truckload of heartache and recriminations.

She'd do well to keep her distance until she figured out more about Dean Harding.

"No, thanks," she said. "I'd better let my supper settle first."

"Guess it'll be just you and me, Bear." He began to walk toward the open meadow.

"Wait!"

He turned back toward her. "Change your mind?"

Her heart pounding in her throat, she pointed at the

path to the spring. Her mother, straw hat askew, bare legs pumping, was racing toward her.

Alone.

Kate ran to meet her, only barely aware of Dean following close behind. "Where's Mikey?"

"Gone." Shelley's face crumpled in distress. "I can't find him anywhere."

CHAPTER THREE

"I LOOKED EVERYWHERE." Shelley panted for breath and made an obvious effort not to cry. "When I couldn't find him, I came back here, hoping he'd returned to you."

Dean glanced from the high color of Shelley's face to the panic in Kate's brown eyes. If he didn't take control, in a few minutes he would have not only a lost little boy but a couple of hysterical women on his hands.

"Mrs. Purvis," he said, "do you have a cell phone?"

She nodded. "In my purse."

"Good. You wait here in case Mikey returns. Kate and I will look for him. If we're not back in fifteen minutes, call the police and report him missing. Okay?"

Shelley collapsed on the picnic bench, swept off her straw hat and fanned her face with it. "Shouldn't I help you search?"

"Dean's right," Kate said. "Someone should be here in case Mikey wanders back."

If he hadn't noted the fear clouding her deep brown eyes, the rapid pulse in the slender column of her neck, Dean would have sworn Kate was calm and collected. As a doctor, she was used to life-and-death emergencies, but she was a mother, too, and her only child was missing. He respected her composure, guessing how much it cost her to appear calm for her mother's sake.

"Where did you see Mikey last?" Dean asked.

Shelley's lower lip trembled. "Right before we reached the entrance to the springs. I stopped to speak with Mrs. Filbert—she's a neighbor. When I turned back to Mikey, he was gone."

Dean checked his watch. "Fifteen minutes, then call 911, okay?"

"Don't worry about me," Shelley said. "Just hurry, find Mikey."

Dean whistled to Bear, who fell in step beside him on one side, Kate on the other. Together they headed at a rapid pace in the direction of the springs.

"Has Mikey done this before?" he asked.

"Wandered off on his own?" Kate's sharp gaze scanned the park. "No, he knows better. He wouldn't have left his Nana unless—"

Her horrified expression said it all. He could read her worst fears as if they were emblazoned on her forehead.

"Boys don't always do as they're told," Dean reassured her, "even good boys."

She attempted a smile and arched an eyebrow at him. "Speaking from experience?"

"You bet." He grinned, hoping to ease her tension. "I've done my share of hell-raising. We're probably going to find Mikey with a group of kids, having the time of his life.''

God, he hoped so, but his police experience taunted him with statistics, with memories of cases of children who disappeared, never to be seen again, or worse yet, were found dead, tortured, molested. He shook the gruesome possibilities away. The kid was probably playing in the springs, cannonballing with others his age, oblivious to the terror his absence was inflicting on his mother and grandmother.

''Does Mikey swim?'' he asked.

Kate's lovely face paled beneath the pink of her exertion. ''He's just learning. You don't think—''

''We'll check the springs first.''

They searched diligently among the tall pecans and cottonwoods that cast long shadows in the early evening sunshine, hopes rising at the sight of every little boy in a striped T-shirt, only to be dashed when the child was someone else's. Although the sun was close to setting, the smothering heat of the Texas day lingered, rising off the pathways and made bearable only by the persistent gentle breeze. Dean and Kate passed several more groups of children, but Mikey wasn't with any of them.

When they reached the entrance to the springs, Dean eyed *Philosophers' Rock,* a sculpture depicting past literary and historical giants of Texas: Walter Prescott Webb, Roy Bedicek, and J. Frank Dobie. Dean recalled the well-worn volume of Dobie's *Tales of Old-Time Texas* that lay on the nightstand beside his bed at the ranch. That book had helped him through many a sleepless night.

Nights without Maggie.

The old bitterness seeped through him, crept up his throat, threatened to choke him. If only the damned doctors had been on their toes, caught the cancer in time, he'd have his Maggie. He'd still be working as a cop and living in San Antonio, looking forward to going home every night, swinging Maggie into his arms, and talking about the day they'd start a family, have children of their own.

Children.

He jerked his thoughts back to Mikey Purvis. The boy's mother was a member of that fraternity of so-called healers who had missed the obvious and let Maggie die, but Kate Purvis didn't deserve the terror she was experiencing now. Losing a child topped the list of worst nightmares in his book.

With Kate at his side, Dean paced the nine-hundred-foot length of the spring-fed pool, checking the water and the banks for a glimpse of the cute five-year-old. The sounds of splashing water, shouts and laughter, and the rustle of cottonwood leaves filled the air. Some visitors to the springs sprawled on towels on the grassy slopes, others waded in the chilly water at the pool's shallow end. A few perched on rocks at the far end of the pool, but there was no sign of a little boy with sun-streaked brown hair, eyes like his mother, and a grin that could light up a room.

Dean headed toward the deep end of the pool with Kate on his heels.

"He wouldn't come here," she insisted. "He always promised to stay in the shallow end."

Having once been a boy himself, Dean knew nothing was more enticing than the forbidden. "Won't hurt to check."

They found the deep end crowded with teenagers. Dean stopped one of them on the grassy slope, a young girl with pale skin and a bikini that left nothing to the imagination. "Have you seen a little boy around here, five years old, brown hair and brown eyes?"

The girl shook her head. "Most folks don't allow their little kids at this end. It's fourteen feet deep, plus some of those guys—" she nodded toward a group of teenaged boys roughhousing on the water's edge "—play kinda rough."

Kate gasped. "You don't think—"

The girl looked at her with sympathy. "They're good guys. They wouldn't hurt a kid. They'd just run him off."

Dean thanked the girl and turned to Kate. "If he was here, he's already left. We'd better check the rest of the park."

Without a word, Kate pivoted on her heel and hurried toward the entrance. Dean had to hustle to keep up. With her thick brown hair caught up in a ponytail, a navy-blue pullover that molded her small, perfect breasts, and crisp white shorts and spotless sneakers that showed off her long, tanned legs, Kate could have passed for one of the teenagers they'd just left— except for the maturity and experience that had sculpted her face with remarkable beauty and a seductive poignancy.

Fear for her son emanated from her like a palpable distress signal, and Dean struggled to remain objective. He didn't want to like the woman. In the first place, she was a doctor, a profession that ranked just above pond scum on his list. And in the second, he found the lies and deception his job required easier when he kept her at arm's length. But beneath the veneer of professional competency, he'd sensed a vulnerability that intrigued him and kindled his protective instincts. Keeping his distance kept getting a whole lot harder.

They exited the springs and turned toward the section of park they hadn't searched yet. Daylight was fading fast, and he could sense Kate's panic rising with the failing light.

She glanced at him with glistening eyes. "If somebody took him, they're way ahead of us by now."

Dean stopped abruptly, grabbed her by the upper arms, and shook her slightly. "Don't go there. You'll drive yourself crazy. We could find him playing with friends around the next curve."

She made a visible effort to pull herself together. "You're right. I'll be no help finding him if I let my imagination run rampant."

She inhaled a long shivering breath, and he felt her relax beneath his grip. Her skin was soft and warm, her muscles firm. With reluctance, he let her go.

"It's been almost half an hour since your mother

called them in," he said. "The police are already searching by now."

"But if they don't know what he looks like—"

"I'm sure Shelley gave them a description, along with the details of what he's wearing. Cops are trained observers. They'll find him."

Without slowing her pace, she threw him a questioning glance. "You know a lot about police procedure."

He cursed beneath his breath. In his desire to reassure her, he'd revealed too much. "Television. Can't get enough of those police dramas."

She nodded and attempted a smile. "I suppose policemen love cowboy shows."

Keeping a steady pace and observing each small boy they passed, he threw her a question. If he could keep her talking about trivia, maybe she'd concentrate less on her fears. "What about you?"

"What *about* me?" Her face had lit up at the sight of a small boy in a striped shirt, but when the child turned to face her, he was obviously not her son. Disappointment seemed to drain the light from her exquisite face.

"You watch medical dramas?" he asked.

She shook her head. "I don't have time for TV, unless I watch a Disney video on the weekend with Mikey." Her words caught in her throat, and when she spoke again, her voice was husky. "I'll never forgive myself for not spending more time with him."

"Don't beat up on yourself. I've seen you in action.

You're a great mom.'' Dean reached for her hand and squeezed it gently. "We'll find him."

He wished he felt as confident as he sounded. From experience, he knew the more time passed, the less likely they were to find Mikey at all—or to recover him unharmed. Kate Purvis was a strong woman, but a good part of her strength came from her love of family. Losing Mikey would devastate her.

"Hey!" a deep male voice shouted behind them. "Dean, is that you?"

Dean glanced over his shoulder. A uniformed police officer was jogging up the path toward him. Recognizing the man's face, Dean inhaled sharply. Roger McSwain was one of his former partners on the San Antonio police force.

"Hi, Rog." Dean stopped and held out his hand. "Haven't seen you in a while."

McSwain shook his hand and grinned. "I didn't know you were in Austin. I thought—"

"I'm here looking for work as a carpenter," Dean interrupted before McSwain could say more.

McSwain frowned. "A carpenter? But you—"

"You on the lookout for the lost kid?" Dean asked.

"Yeah. Several of us are combing the park." The short, stocky cop rubbed a meaty hand across his sweaty face. "You searching, too?"

Dean nodded and turned to Kate. "This is Mikey's mother, Dr. Kate Purvis. We've checked the springs and the other side of the park. No sign of him."

McSwain nodded. "We'll find your boy," he assured Kate, then looked back to Dean. "Son of a gun, man, I haven't seen you since—"

"It's been a long time." Dean narrowed his eyes and flashed the cop a warning signal. "Officer McSwain and I graduated from high school together in San Antonio," he lied to Kate, and prayed Roger wouldn't correct him.

McSwain wrinkled his reddened face in an instant of confusion, but he didn't contradict Dean. "Good to see you again, Dean. We're doing everything we can to find your son, Dr. Purvis." Touching the tips of his fingers to his cap, the officer moved past them.

Dean could feel Kate staring at him, but he didn't return her puzzled gaze. "Let's keep moving while there's still light left."

TEN MINUTES LATER, they had almost reached the end of the park farthest from the picnic area. Kate tugged on Dean's sleeve. "I've got to take a breather. Your legs are longer than mine."

He stopped beside a park bench, and she collapsed gratefully, sucking in air. She had pushed her body as hard as she could, hoping and praying to find Mikey just around another bend in the path or among the next group of kids, but so far, nothing. She tried hard not to cry. Tears wouldn't help Mikey now. She had to recover her energy and keep moving.

Her heart pounded wildly in her chest and she guessed her blood pressure was elevated as well, as much from fear as from exertion. Even with a mischievous streak a mile wide, Mikey was an obedient child. He *knew* better than to wander off from his nana or mother. He wouldn't have gone off on his own. Someone had taken him.

Stop it, she argued with herself. *You keep thinking that way and you'll drive yourself crazy.*

Maybe Mikey had strayed away with a friend, with some other family he'd met in the park. She stifled a sob that threatened to break through her lips. He *had* to be all right. She couldn't accept any other alternative.

Dean Harding sat beside her on the bench, mercifully quiet. She couldn't have spoken past the lump in her throat. Bear came forward and placed his head on her knee in a canine gesture of solace.

"You okay?" Dean asked.

His eyes held a tenderness and concern she hadn't noted before, and she had a momentary desire to drown herself in the comfort of their soft gray depths. He slipped his arm around her shoulder and hugged her against the hard muscles of his chest. His touch was warm, nurturing, a balm to her raw nerves and aching heart.

"We'll find him," he assured her. "If we have to turn Austin upside down and inside out, we'll find him."

The fervor of his promise made her a believer. She breathed deeply, willing the stitch in her side to ease, her racing pulse to slow, and her nostrils filled with the scent of the man beside her. He smelled of fresh-cut grass, sunshine and clean male sweat, and she longed to lay her head on his chest and let him take care of her. She'd been lonely for so long, and now, without Mikey, she was even more alone.

Without Mikey!

With a jerk, she pushed to her feet. How could she be thinking of Dean Harding when Mikey was missing? What kind of mother was she? She felt her face flush with remorse. If she'd gone to the springs with Mikey and her mother, her son wouldn't have disappeared. If she hadn't remained behind to talk with the fascinating cowboy who'd entered her life so suddenly and unexpectedly, Mikey would now be safe at home. She hoped wherever he was, he was with friends. She couldn't bear to think of him lost and alone, or worse, in the company of a stranger who frightened him.

Guilt stabbed through her like a freshly honed scalpel. She was a woman with needs and interests of her own, but the day the doctor had placed that tiny, red and wrinkled bundle in her arms, she had become first and foremost a mother. No man could divert her from that responsibility, a commitment born of love and nurtured by five of the happiest years of her life. She shut her mind to the magnetism of the man at her side and started down the path on her own.

Dean caught up with her easily, and Bear ran ahead of them.

"You'd better pace yourself," Dean said. "It could be a long search."

"How can I not hurry? He's *my* son," she shouted.

"Nobody said he wasn't," Dean replied with a reasonableness that brought another flush to her face. His smoky gray eyes seemed to see right through her, gauging her guilt, measuring her desperation.

"Sorry," she muttered. "I didn't mean to snap."

"No offense taken. I'd say you're holding up remarkably well under the circumstances." He stood like a bulwark between her and complete panic.

She couldn't force a smile. "That's because you can't hear the hysteria and self-recrimination inside my head."

He reached for her hand and squeezed it gently. "It's been less than an hour since he disappeared. Some cop has probably already picked Mikey up and he's waiting for you at the station, having ice cream."

His words gave her fresh hope and she threw him a grateful glance, noting the kind expression on his rugged face.

"There's a pay phone at the park entrance not far ahead," she said. "We can call the police station from there."

Hope revitalized her tired muscles, and she strode quickly along the path, taking two steps for every one of Dean's long strides. In front of them, Bear stopped occasionally to sniff the path, then bounded on ahead.

"Can he pick up Mikey's scent?" Kate asked.

"It's possible. Labs are often used as search-and-rescue dogs."

"So he could be following Mikey's trail?"

Dean shrugged with a wry grin. "Or he could be stalking a squirrel."

As she scanned the park and the few people remaining in the waning light, Kate couldn't help thinking what an enigma Dean Harding was. He'd told her very little about himself, and she couldn't help wondering whether he was just the most uncommunicative man she'd ever met or if he was hiding something. He was a fascinating paradox. One minute he was comforting and considerate, the next abrupt and almost rude. His encounter with his former high school classmate had left her feeling he couldn't wait to get away from Roger McSwain. Had Dean been that anxious to return to their search, or had he feared McSwain might reveal his secrets?

If Dean Harding had secrets, what were they?

Reining in her straying thoughts, she focused on Bear. The dog's nose was to the ground as she followed a scent at a gentle lope.

"What is it, girl?" Dean called. "Have you found Mikey?"

Bear stopped, turned in a circle, wagged her tail and barked with exuberance.

Dean grabbed Kate's arm and pulled her forward. "That's Bear talk for *yes*. Let's go."

Kate ran beside Dean as they followed the dog out of the park. Even though rush hour had long passed, traffic whizzed by on the busy street. Bear rushed to the curb and stopped.

"Oh, no," Kate cried. "She's lost him."

"Maybe not," Dean said as they caught up with the animal, who was pacing at the street's edge. "She's a smart dog. She knows better than to dart into traffic."

He leaned over and scratched Bear behind the ears. "Which way, girl?"

Bear faced the street and barked.

"We'll have to cross." Dean took Kate's arm. "Heel, Bear."

At the next break in traffic, they dashed across the street. Bear ran in circles on the sidewalk, nose to the ground, then headed up the pavement away from the park. Running as fast as she could to keep up, Kate followed Dean and his dog.

Halfway up the block, she glanced toward the intersection. A city bus had pulled alongside the curb, and a line of people were climbing aboard. Kate's heart lurched as she spied Mikey, his hand held by a young man whose face Kate couldn't see.

"Hurry, Dean," she called. "It's Mikey! He's getting on the bus."

With a burst of speed that left her far behind, Dean sprinted toward the bus stop. Bear raced at his heels, barking at the top of her lungs.

Kate watched in horror as Mikey and the stranger stepped on the bus. The doors closed, and the bus pulled away in a cloud of diesel fumes just as Dean reached the corner.

Mikey was gone.

CHAPTER FOUR

"MIKEY!"

Kate's scream reverberated in Dean's ears along with Bear's frantic barking. The pain and terror in her voice pierced him like a serrated knife. Leaning forward, hands on his thighs, he sucked air, cursing silently. He'd failed her and that adorable little boy. He'd been so close, but he'd lost Mikey and the mysterious young man who had abducted him.

"Do you have a cell phone?" he asked as Kate reached him.

"Only my beeper."

Hysteria lay just beneath the surface of her voice, her thick, fine hair blew in tangles around her heart-shaped face, and tears glistened in her brown eyes. Even in distress, she was one of the most beautiful women he'd ever seen. He wanted to gather her in his arms and comfort her, but it wasn't the time or place. They had to stay on Mikey's trail.

She twirled in a circle, checking the sidewalks on both sides of the street. "And there's no sign of a pay phone."

The light had changed just as the bus pulled away, and a battered white pickup with a C and J Construction logo stopped at the intersection. Rap music blasted from its radio speakers, and its engine revved impatiently. The driver, dressed in work clothes, leaned toward the open passenger window.

"Saw you folks miss the bus," he called over the raucous blast of music. "Need a ride?"

Dean didn't hesitate. He motioned Bear into the truck bed and wrenched open the passenger door for Kate. They barely had time to settle on the cab's bench seat before the light changed, and the man floored the accelerator.

"This is Dr. Purvis," Dean yelled to the driver over the roar of rap. "Her son's been kidnapped, and he's on that bus. Can you catch up with it?"

"Damn, lady." The driver's dark eyes glistened with sympathy and he punched a control on the dash, shutting off the racket. "That's awful."

"Can you catch the bus?" Dean repeated.

The driver broke into a wide grin that exposed gleaming white teeth and one flashing gold incisor. "This old rust bucket don't look like much, but she carries a ton of horsepower. We'll get that bus or my name's not Sam Oats."

"Go for it, Sam," Dean said. "That little boy's counting on you. So's his mom."

Sam shifted gears, and the truck picked up speed. Dean could just make out the bus far ahead of them in the snarl of heavy traffic. It hadn't stopped since picking up Mikey. He glanced at Kate. She sat stiffly, one hand braced against the dashboard. A fine line of white etched her tight lips, and her other hand clenched her knee, the pale-pink nails biting into her skin. She was holding herself together, but only barely.

"We've almost got him," Dean said in a soothing tone. "It's just a matter of time."

As if his words had jinxed them, Sam's truck was caught at the next light.

"Don't stop!" Kate cried. "If you get a ticket, I'll pay for it."

Sam shook his head. "Won't do your boy no good if I get us killed, ma'am. Too much traffic on the cross street. I run that light, somebody'll T-bone us for sure."

Dean heard Kate bite back a whimper as the bus disappeared ahead of them. "We'll catch it," he assured her. He covered her hand with his and was startled by the coldness of her flesh. "The bus has to stop sooner or later to take on or let off passengers."

The light changed and Sam stomped on the gas pedal. The old pickup roared ahead, but Dean still couldn't locate the bus.

"Oh, no," Kate groaned. "The road."

Dean swore under his breath. The wide boulevard forked ahead of them, and they couldn't see the bus down either branch of the heavily traveled thoroughfare. The bus would have plenty of time to stop and Mikey's abductor could disappear into a neighborhood with the child before Dean and Kate could catch up. Now that he knew Mikey had actually been kidnapped, his fears for the boy escalated. He had to nab

Mikey getting off the bus or Kate might never see her son again.

Alive.

"Which way?" Sam asked.

Dean hesitated only an instant. "Left. The right fork leads downtown. I'm guessing a kidnapper would head for the suburbs."

"Left, it is." With a vicious jerk of the steering wheel, Sam forced his way into the left stream of traffic.

Horns honked behind them, and from the outside rearview mirror, Dean caught one driver making obscene gestures. Road rage was the least of his worries. He prayed he'd guessed right. When he'd worked on the police force, his instincts had been good. He hoped he still had what it took to think like a criminal. He couldn't bear facing Kate if they lost Mikey.

Sam Oats drove like a maniac, weaving in and out of traffic like a movie stuntman in a high-speed chase. Dean glanced out the rear window and caught a glimpse of Bear, paws braced on the truck bed, ears back, fur blowing in the wind and her mouth open in a silly dog grin. At least somebody was enjoying this.

Kate gripped his arm. "There's a bus. Is it the same one?"

Dean peered through the throng of cars and SUVs on the road in front of them. He could barely make out the number on the bus. "It's the one!"

"Can you get behind it, Sam?" Kate shouted above the roar of the pickup's engine.

Dean prayed under his breath that the bus hadn't

had time for a quick stop to disgorge passengers while they'd lost sight of it.

"Hang on." Sam swerved into the right lane, forcing his truck into line directly behind the bus. Exhaust fumes filled the cab, causing Dean's eyes to water. Beside him, Kate coughed, fighting for breath, but not taking her eyes off the road ahead.

The bus's brake lights flashed.

"It's stopping." Sam pulled to the curb behind the bus, and before the truck had completely slowed, Kate was tumbling out the door and racing toward the front end of the bus, screaming her son's name like a madwoman.

"Find a phone and call the police," Dean shouted over his shoulder to Sam as he followed Kate, Bear at his heels, her frantic barking mixing with Kate's cries above the roar of traffic.

The bus doors opened with a pneumatic hiss. Mikey and the stranger stepped off and headed away from Kate.

"Mikey!" she screamed, never slowing her steps.

The boy stopped and turned at the sound of his mother's voice. His cherubic face lit up in a joyful smile and he waved with his free hand. "Mommy!"

Bear lunged ahead and locked his jaws on the stranger's pant leg.

That break in the pair's momentum gave Dean enough time to reach them. He passed Kate on the run and brought down the stranger with a flying tackle, tumbling with the man to the sidewalk and landing on top of him.

LATER THAT NIGHT, Dean adjusted the ice pack on his aching knee, sipped tepid coffee, and thought longingly of the bottle of Jack Daniel's in the suitcase beneath his bed upstairs. Glancing up at the sound of footsteps, he watched Kate enter the parlor and collapse in the chair across from his. Although exhausted, she moved with elegance and grace, and her tiredness did nothing to detract from the delicate beauty of her face. Amazed, he found himself wanting to rise and go to her, to wrap his arms around her, to comfort—

Fatigue must be making him crazy. With effort, he squelched his provocative thoughts and worked to keep them from showing in his expression. "Mikey okay?"

With a rueful smile, she shoved her fingers through her thick hair, pushing it off her face. "Sleeping like a rock. He thinks the whole ordeal was some kind of adventure."

"And your mother?"

Worry flickered through her brown eyes, setting his protective instincts on alert again. "I gave her a sedative. She blames herself for everything."

He didn't dare touch her, too afraid of where that seductive contact might lead, but he could comfort her with words. "She knows Mikey's safe now. That's all that matters."

Kate turned the corners of her alluring mouth downward in a grimace. "Tell that to Peter Tirrell."

Dean thought back to tackling the stranger who'd taken Mikey off the bus. He and Kate had been amazed to discover Shelley's shy boarder was the man with Mikey.

Dean frowned. "I thought Tirrell was all right."

"He has cuts and abrasions—and a sore shoulder where you jerked his arm behind him, but otherwise, he's fine. I cleaned and bandaged his scrapes and gave him something for pain. But he's angry at being unjustly accused." The silky skin of her forehead wrinkled with concern, and his fingers itched to smooth the creases away.

"I'm hoping he won't file charges against you for assault," Kate added.

Her words jerked him from his contemplation of her. Tirrell was thinking of suing him? That did it. Dean laid aside the ice pack and pushed to his feet. "Don't move. I'll be right back."

Wincing from the pain in his knee, an old football injury exacerbated by his sprint after the bus and leap at Peter Tirrell, he climbed the stairs and retrieved the bottle of Jack Daniel's. Stopping by the kitchen on his way back to the parlor, he tucked the bottle under his arm, grabbed a couple of glasses, and filled them with ice from the dispenser in the refrigerator door.

Kate looked up when he entered the parlor again. "What's this?"

"Medicine," Dean said with a wry grin. He set the glasses on the table between them, poured liberally from the bottle and handed her a glass. "Just what the doctor ordered."

She raised a feathery eyebrow and flashed him a teasing smile that sent his pulse pounding. "Practicing medicine without a license? I could have you arrested.''

He settled into his chair, replaced the ice pack on the red-hot poker stabbing his knee, and lifted his glass in a silent toast. ''Add impersonating a doctor to the assault charge. Maybe I can find an attorney who'll give me a discount rate.''

Her companionable smile filled him with satisfaction and an unaccustomed warmth—or maybe the heat came from the smooth whiskey flooding his bloodstream. Whatever the cause, he was happy she'd thrown off the pinched, panicked look she'd worn throughout the search for Mikey. She hadn't lost it immediately once they'd found the boy, though, not until she'd assured herself that he was emotionally and physically unharmed.

She sipped tentatively at her drink. ''Will the police be back?''

He shook his head. ''They seemed satisfied with what Mikey and Peter told them. I doubt the police will file charges against Tirrell.''

She leaned against the back of the chair and closed her eyes, dark lashes sweeping her smooth skin. ''It was all so bizarre.''

Dean couldn't argue with her assessment. When the police had arrived on the scene after Sam Oats's call and lifted the struggling, cursing kidnapper from the pavement, Kate had gasped in surprise and recognition.

''Peter Tirrell,'' she said. ''He's our boarder.''

"He was taking me home, Mommy," Mikey insisted. "I lost Nana in the park, and Peter found me."

Peter's pale complexion was livid with anger and his hay-colored hair stood in spikes as he jerked his clothing into place. He glared at Dean, anger sparking in his watery blue eyes. "That's a hell of a thank-you for saving the kid. Who knows what kind of pervert might have found him if I hadn't come along?"

The officers had driven them all to the station, where they'd isolated Mikey and Peter and questioned them separately. From what Dean had gathered later from the detective in charge, Mikey's story had matched Peter's. The boy had lost sight of his grandmother, Peter had found him, and they were supposedly headed home when Dean and Kate intercepted them.

There had been a major flaw in the story. The bus Peter had taken was headed away from Shelley's boardinghouse, not toward it. Peter had explained that having lived in Austin only a few weeks, he'd become disoriented. When he'd realized the bus was going in the wrong direction, he and Mikey had disembarked to catch a bus that would take them home. That's when Dean had jumped him.

Dean looked up to find Kate staring at him. With one leg curled beneath her, her hair still in disarray from their wild chase, and her wide eyes glistening with anxiety, she projected a vulnerability that almost made him forget he hated doctors. She almost made him forget, too, the real reason he was there in her house. He sighed inwardly. He'd have to wait at least another night to further his investigation, and the delay wasn't going to make Mitch Barnes happy. Mitch wanted to find the mother of his child, and Dylan had hired Dean to do it quickly.

"Do you think Peter was telling the truth?" Kate asked.

Dean thought for a moment before answering. His instincts prevented him from fully buying Tirrell's story, but he had no solid evidence against the young man. "The cops checked him out in the national crime computers. Tirrell has no record. No sexual perversion, not even a speeding ticket. The guy's as clean as they come."

Her hand shook, rattling the ice in her glass, and she grasped the tumbler with both hands to quiet it. "Then why don't I feel reassured?"

"Because you're a mother." His heart ached for her. She'd been to hell and back that day, and for her, the anxiety still wasn't over. As long as she was Mikey's mother, the apprehension would *never* be over. "Mothers always worry about their kids. Didn't they teach you that in your obstetrics courses? There's a species-specific gene called mother worrywart. All women have it. My mother had it in triplicate."

His attempt at humor worked and coaxed a smile from her. She finished her drink, set her glass aside, and stood. "I'm heading for bed." She nodded toward his knee. "You want something for the pain before I go?"

He wanted something all right, but it had nothing to do with the soreness in his knee. His ache was a bit higher and more centered. "No, thanks. Ice is the best thing for it."

He suppressed a grin at the irony of his remedy. Ice or a cold shower. Either would effectively cure the longing in his groin. He pushed himself to his feet and faced her. "You'd better get some sleep. You've had a rough day."

"You, too." She tilted her head and gazed up at him, rosy lips slightly parted, her cheeks flushed from Jack Daniel's, her bourbon-colored eyes dreamy with fatigue. "I never thanked you properly—"

"It's okay." The faint lilac scent of her perfume tantalized him. "Besides, Bear deserves the credit. She did the tracking."

Kate grinned. "Bear gets sirloin for supper tomorrow. My treat."

He couldn't stop himself from brushing a wayward tendril of hair from her forehead. The silky smoothness of her skin disarmed him, and before he could think better of it, he cupped her face in his hands. "You going to be okay?"

"Sure," she insisted, but her voice faltered. Her gaze met his, and again he was stricken by her vulnerability. Kate Purvis was a strong, capable woman who dealt with matters of life and death every day. But when harm had threatened her son, her professional armor had cracked, exposing her maternal feelings, flooding her with fear. Empathy surged through him, and he dipped his lips to hers in a kiss meant solely to comfort.

She tasted of smoky whiskey and a honey flavor

all her own, and the texture of her lips against his fired his senses. Fatigue and alcohol had weakened his defenses, and his gesture of comfort deepened to something more. He threaded his fingers through her thick hair and pulled her toward him. She came, unresisting, and the heat of her burned along the length of him. Her soft breasts crushed against his chest, her bare legs sizzled along his jeans, her hips molded to his.

With a soft moan, she lifted her arms and encircled his neck, her lips opened beneath his, and the room seemed to whirl around them. Long-buried emotions roused and stirred within him, and he reveled in the sensation of being alive, a feeling he hadn't experienced in over five years.

The next instant, she abruptly withdrew her arms, and with the flat of her palms against his chest was pushing him away. Confusion and alarm flashed in her magnificent eyes, and a beguiling shade of red crept up her slender neck and enhanced the color in her cheeks.

She opened her mouth to speak, but closed it again, apparently unsure of what to say.

"Sorry," he said. "I shouldn't have—"

"No apologies." She straightened her spine, visibly gathering her composure. A chilly expression settled across her features, like a door slamming in his face. "It never happened. Good night, Dean."

She pivoted on her heel and marched out of the room as if trying hard not to run.

Dean sank into his chair, poured himself another

drink and bolted it down. "It happened, all right," he muttered to himself in the empty room. "I just wish to hell it hadn't."

His growing attraction to Dr. Kate Purvis could put a decided crimp in his plans.

CHAPTER FIVE

AT THE HOSPITAL the next morning, Kate adjusted the blinds of her office window to block the rising sun, eased herself gingerly onto the sofa, and slapped a cold compress against her forehead.

She was a damned fool.

Yesterday she'd allowed her fascination with a handsome man to distract her from her son. She'd thought she'd learned the lesson from Steven that good-looking men were trouble from the get-go, but, no, she'd cozied up to Dean Harding like a freezing woman to a fire, letting her hormones lead her where her head would never go. And look what it had almost cost her.

If it hadn't been for Peter Tirrell—

A soft knock at her office door and Abby's voice calling her name interrupted her verbal self-flagellation. Without rising from her supine position, Kate lifted one corner of the compress and called in her most irritated tone, "Go away."

The effort cost her, causing a wave of nausea to unsettle her stomach and the sound of her own voice slammed through her head like a tsunami.

Despite her plea, the door opened, and from beneath the edge of her compress, she saw Abby, squinting at her across the dimness of the shuttered room.

"You okay, Kate?"

Kate groaned and settled deeper into the sofa. "Just ducky. Unless you count a whopper of a hangover and an incurable case of terminal stupidity."

Abby sank into the chair beside her, smoothed her white coat and the stethoscope hanging from its pocket, then reached over and patted Kate on the shoulder. Her eyes twinkled and her lips quivered as if she stifled a grin. "Always glad to hear you're well."

Kate scowled, then winced at the pain it caused her. Even the muscles in her face ached. "Nothing like a kindly dose of sympathy from a friend to perk me right up."

Abby's expression sobered. "Want to tell me what drove you to tie one on?"

"Not what. Who."

"Okay, then. Who?"

"I only had one drink. You know how sensitive I am to alcohol. One sip and I'm snookered."

Abby lifted an eyebrow. "You know that, too. So how come you fell victim to demon rum?"

"Whiskey. Jack Daniel's."

Abby leaned closer. "Strong stuff. That definitely explains the bloodshot eyes—"

Moaning, Kate lay back on the sofa and readjusted the compress to block out the light. "Do you have to talk so loud? The slightest noise is like a spike through my brain.''

"Are you going to tell me what happened?" Abby asked in a softer tone.

"I made a complete and utter fool of myself yesterday, and it almost cost me Mikey.''

"You're kidding!"

Kate winced at the volume of Abby's outburst, then shook her head. The movement sent more waves of nausea washing over her. "I wish."

Swallowing against the bile that threatened to rise in her throat, Kate filled Abby in on the whole story, from Dean Harding's arrival as a boarder, to the picnic and Mikey's disappearance, and finally to his return and the "capture" of Peter Tirrell.

"Good God," Abby muttered. "I thought I was doing you a favor by having someone cover for you to have an evening off. Sounds like a nightmare.''

"Believe me, I'd be in better shape this morning if I'd just come off a forty-eight-hour shift.''

"You still haven't explained where Jack Daniel's came in.''

Kate felt herself flush beneath the cold cloth on her forehead. "Dean gave it to me."

"He was trying to get you drunk?" Abby sounded outraged.

"Of course not. He doesn't know my hypersensitivity to liquor. He thought it would help.''

"Help? As in loosening up your inhibitions?"

"Abby!"

"Face it, Kate. You *are* something of an ice

maiden where men are concerned. I just figured the guy was trying to thaw you out a bit.''

''I don't need thawing out!''

''Glad to hear it. So what happened *after* Jack Daniel's appeared on the scene?''

''I kissed him.''

''Jack Daniel's?''

The cloth still covered Kate's eyes but she could hear the laughter in Abby's voice. If it hadn't hurt to move, Kate would have smacked her.

''I kissed Dean Harding! I told you I was suffering from terminal stupidity.''

''What's stupid about a kiss? I'm rather fond of them myself.''

''That's because you have a very handsome and extremely respectable husband who loves you.''

''He hasn't always been my husband—and we had to start somewhere.''

''But Dean Harding is different!''

''Is he handsome?''

Kate groaned and slid lower onto the sofa. ''Incredibly.''

''Respectable?''

Kate thought for a moment. ''I don't have the faintest idea. The man's a drifter without a job. All he seems to have to his name is a pickup truck and a lovable dog.''

''Didn't you just tell me he helped search for Mikey? That he threw himself at the alleged kidnapper and took him down?''

Kate wiggled uncomfortably. ''Yes, but—''

"And when he kissed you, did he force himself on you, make unwanted advances?"

Just remembering the slow, easy grace of that kiss, which had filled her with an instant phosphorescence, made her body tingle. "No."

"Then I don't see how you can claim stupidity," Abby said with annoying reasonableness.

"I can't go around kissing a total stranger," Kate insisted.

"Then get to know him better."

Her eyes covered by the cold cloth, Kate couldn't see Abby's face, but she could hear the smile in her voice. "Why? So I can fall in love and have my heart broken when he moves on, like Steven did? Fool me once, shame on you. Fool me twice, shame on me."

"Maybe if he gets to know you better, he won't move on. He might decide you're a damned good reason to hang around."

Kate shook her head. "Don't go there. What would the two of us have in common?"

"Great sex?"

That did it. Kate yanked the compress from her forehead and tossed it at Abby, catching her by surprise with a wet cloth across the face.

Laughing, Abby removed the soggy material and dropped it on the table beside the sofa. "You've been alone too long, Kate. I'm not saying you need a man to be happy, but having a good one around has lots of advantages. Just get to know your cowboy better. There could be more to him than meets the eye. You might find you do have things in common."

Roses, Kate thought, remembering the day Dean had appeared at her door. She slammed her mind shut against the memories. She'd fallen in love before, and it had brought her nothing but heartache. She didn't want things in common with Dean Harding. She wanted armor against his appeal, a security system to guard her heart.

Abby's look softened. "There's more to life than work, girl, but you have to take a chance. Just because you enjoy a handsome man's company doesn't mean you're going to fall in love with him. Just have a good time."

Kate pursed her lips thoughtfully. Abby's words made sense, but her friend hadn't met Dean Harding, didn't know that beneath that howdy-ma'am, aw-shucks casual charm resided a depth that scared her. Somehow Kate knew he wasn't a man who indulged in light flirtations.

"Now," Abby ordered, "stop by my office before you start your rounds. I have just the cure for that hangover."

Abby slipped out the door as quietly as she entered. Kate didn't doubt her friend had something to ease her headache. Abby had a cure for practically everything.

Except a broken heart.

No way, Kate decided, was she running that risk again.

THAT NIGHT, Dean sat in his room on the second floor of Shelley's boardinghouse and listened to the sounds of activity outside his door. Bear stretched out on a rug at his feet, her ears pricked as she, too, gauged the comings and goings in the household.

The bottle of Jack Daniel's stood on the table beside his bed, but Dean had sworn off whiskey tonight. He needed a clear head and steady hands for the job ahead. Besides, the taste of it would bring back too clearly the flavor of Kate's kiss from the night before, a memory too enticing for a man with a mission who was just passing through.

He knew he'd somehow offended her. This morning he'd risen early, made coffee, and waited in the kitchen for her to appear. He'd intended to apologize for his boldness, to promise he wouldn't let it happen again. She hadn't given him the chance. He'd heard her descend the stairs, but instead of stopping for coffee, she'd headed straight out the door.

Tonight she'd missed dinner, coming in only after everyone else had finished. At first he'd guessed she was still avoiding him, but she'd explained there'd been a difficult delivery at the hospital. She'd almost lost the baby, but now mother and premature daughter were doing fine. When Kate had followed Felicity into the kitchen, where the older woman had kept her dinner warm, Dean had noted the deepening violet smudges under Kate's eyes, the fine white lines of fatigue that bracketed her mouth, and the tired slump of her delicate shoulders. She had put in a fifteen-hour day.

He pictured her now, asleep upstairs, curled on her side with one arm tucked beneath her pillow, her dark hair fanned out on the pillowcase like mahogany silk—

Squelching the tenderness her weary appearance had generated, he turned instead to a review of his purpose. He'd decided he couldn't delay his search any longer. Her exhaustion meant Kate would sleep well tonight, which would suit his plans just fine.

Dean checked his watch. Twelve-thirty. He crept to the door of his room and eased it open. No light shone beneath the closed door of Peter Tirrell's room at the front of the house. That meant the computer whiz had finally called it a night. An hour earlier, Raoul had performed his ablutions in the bathroom he shared with Dean, and now his room, too, was quiet. Naomi's room was across the hall, but she'd announced at dinner that she wouldn't be home until the wee hours of the morning. The cast planned to celebrate the opening night of the play and would party until the morning editions of the Austin papers appeared with their reviews.

Dean tiptoed to the foot of the stairs that led to the third floor where the Purvis family slept. Only darkness and quiet reigned at the top of the steps.

Satisfied everyone was asleep, he returned to his room, groped beneath the mattress for his tools, and slipped them, a pair of latex gloves, and a small flashlight in his pockets. Motioning Bear to follow, he descended the stairs to the first floor and moved cautiously toward the kitchen. If Felicity intercepted him, he could always claim he'd come for a midnight snack.

When he reached the kitchen door, he could hear the rumbles of Felicity's snores reverberating through her closed bedroom door just down the hall. Quickly, he dropped to his knees before the door of Kate's office and pulled on the latex gloves. If he was lucky enough to find Terry Monteverde's file, he didn't want Kate discovering it gone, calling in the police, and them nailing him with his prints all over a room he supposedly had never entered. With a few deft movements and the skill of long practice, he disengaged the lock. Within seconds, he and Bear had slipped inside and shut the door behind them.

Dean flicked on the small flashlight and surveyed the room. The office wasn't anything like the cold and clinical setting he'd expected. In fact, it didn't look like an office at all. More like a cozy sitting room with its deep comfortable chair by the fireplace, a braided rug on the floor, and an antique Chippendale table that served as a desk. Bookshelves lined one wall, but only a handful of volumes were medical texts. Most were well-read copies of both classics and popular novels. He checked a few titles and authors and was surprised to find Kate Purvis shared his taste in books.

The room had Kate written all over it. Her warmth, her personality, and an inviting coziness. Being inside was like having Kate wrap her arms around him. He shook away the enticing thought and went to work.

Moving silently but swiftly, he checked the contents of the desk drawers without disturbing them, but could find no references to any of Kate's cases or

patients, much less any trace of Terry Monteverde and
her baby. With dismay, he realized there wasn't even
a filing cabinet in the room—until a boxy table covered with a brocade cloth caught his eye. Lifting the
table skirt, he discovered a two-drawer filing cabinet
concealed beneath.

Thumbing quickly through the file folders, he
found household bills, insurance policies, Mikey's
birth certificate and other personal papers, but nothing
related to Kate's work or her patients. Disappointed,
he closed the file drawers, adjusted the table skirt to
cover the cabinet and left.

In the hall, he reset the dead bolt lock, ripped the
gloves from his hands and shoved them in his pocket
with the lock-picking tools. He'd known that finding
the papers he needed in Kate's home office had been
a long shot, but now his job was a hell of a lot more
difficult. He'd have to access the hospital records to
look for Terry Monteverde's file, and that task would
have to wait until tomorrow.

Another day's delay. Mitch would not be pleased
at the time Dean was taking.

Starting up the hall toward the stairs, he noted a
rhythmic squeak coming from outside. The front door
with its panels of stained glass stood open to the
night, and the breeze caressed his skin. Signaling Bear
to heel, he moved cautiously toward the door and
checked its lock. The mechanism hadn't been forced.

At the door, the creaking sound had increased in
volume, and he realized the noise was coming from
the wicker swing on the far end of the porch. Was it

blowing in the wind? Or had a vagrant taken shelter there for the night?

As soon as he stepped onto the porch he saw her, illuminated by a shaft of moonlight that shot streaks of silver through her brown hair, and bathed her face in a pale luminescence that seemed to emanate from within her. She sat curled in the corner of the swing, one leg folded beneath her, the other pushing against the floor with her bare foot, keeping the swing in motion. Her long, soft sleep shirt clung to the contours of her body, emphasizing the curve of her breasts and the roundness of her hips. With her head thrown back, she gazed past the porch roof to the moon and the few stars visible through the bright lights of Austin. Her posture exposed the slender column of her throat, the entrancing perfection of her profile. In the unearthly light, she could have been a fairy princess or a being from another world, come to weave mystical spells on unsuspecting human men.

For a second, he realized how close he'd come to being discovered. What if Kate had decided to go to her office instead of the porch?

Then the fragrance of night-blooming jasmine swirled around him, adding to the mystical mood, and, with reluctance, he broke the spell by speaking.

"Mind some company?"

Kate flinched at the sound of his voice and drew her other leg beneath her in a defensive posture.

"Sorry," he said. "I didn't mean to frighten you. I came down for a snack, saw the door open and heard the swing. I was just checking to make sure you weren't a burglar.''

"Couldn't sleep."

"After a fifteen-hour workday?''

"I got up to call the hospital to check on my patient. Now I can't go back to sleep."

Dean eased into the wicker rocker nearest the swing. Bear, as if sensing Kate's distress, jumped onto the swing and lay beside her with her head on Kate's lap. Dean started to order the dog off, but Kate reached out and scratched behind Bear's ears, obviously pleased to have the animal close.

"Still worried about your patient?'' Kate's inability to sleep because of concern for her patient didn't jibe with his view of doctors. He'd always found the ones he'd dealt with in Maggie's case cold, clinical and detached.

Heartless bastards.

A tiny hiccup from Kate jerked him from his unhappy memories, and he realized she was trying not to cry. "The mother's fine, but they don't think the infant will survive."

His anger at doctors flared anew. "Shouldn't you be at the hospital with the baby?''

"I wish I could help, but I'm an OB-GYN. I'd only be in the way. The preemie needs a neonatal specialist, and the best one in Austin is with her now."

Dean shifted uneasily in his chair. From their first meeting, Kate had him constantly reassessing his view of the medical profession, and he didn't like the feeling. His self-righteous anger at their incompetence was all that had kept him going after Maggie's death. In a topsy-turvy universe where a good woman had died from a senseless disease, blaming the doctors had been the only satisfactory explanation he could find.

Kate wiped a tear from her cheek with the back of her hand. "I'm sorry. It's not professional of me to get emotionally involved."

"Maybe not professional, but definitely human. You're not a machine," he admitted reluctantly.

Kate continued to stroke Bear's fur. "Emotions get in the way of good treatment. Detachment helps me think more clearly and in the long run is best for the patient. But today I just—"

Her voice trailed off, but she had stoked his curiosity. "What was different about today?"

She was quiet for a moment before answering. "I kept thinking about Mikey, and how I'd felt when he was missing. How terrified I was that something bad had happened to him. I couldn't get that idea out of my mind, so that every patient I saw today wasn't just a patient, but somebody's mother, somebody's child—"

"Somebody's wife." He couldn't keep the anguish from his voice.

"Exactly." She lifted her head to meet his gaze and the tears on her cheeks glistened in the moonlight. "Thank you for understanding."

He understood all right. More than she'd ever guess. And with that understanding came the desire to reach out to her again, to gather her in his arms and comfort her. To kiss the silver tears from her cheeks, to—

If he didn't get a grip on his emotions, he'd never complete this job. "You need rest. You should go to bed. Take one of those sedatives you prescribed for your mother."

His words had come out more brusquely than he'd intended, and she winced visibly at the sharpness in his tone. Exerting all his self-control, he pushed to his feet. "C'mon, Bear. Bedtime for us, old girl."

He tried to walk away without looking back, but when he reached the screen door, his resolve weakened. He turned to where she still sat in the swing.

"Good night, Kate." Cursing the huskiness in his voice, he opened the door and hurried inside before she could reply.

DEAN DIDN'T sleep well that night. Tossing and turning, he tried to devise a plan to gain access to Maitland Maternity's records without setting off any suspicions or alarms—or running into Kate Purvis and blowing his cover.

Finally, at quarter to five, he gave up on both sleep and schemes. After showering and dressing, he descended to the empty kitchen and made coffee. He was in the midst of assembling a western omelette when Kate appeared at the door.

"Coffee smells good," she said.

"Help yourself." He nodded toward the full pot.

From the looks of her, she'd had less sleep than he had. Even though she was dressed in her tailored skirt and blouse, and shoes that in spite of their sensible low heels drew provocative attention to her trim ankles, she looked less like a doctor and more like the attractive woman he was trying like crazy to resist.

"Want some breakfast?" He tried to keep his voice friendly but impersonal, but with Kate looking even more mouthwatering than his omelette, keeping his distance was proving a challenge.

"No time. I'm already running late." She took a mug from the cabinet, filled it to the brim and headed toward the door. "See you later. I'm off to the hospital—"

Her words broke off in a strangled cry. The coffee mug slipped from her fingers, hit the floor, and shattered into pieces.

Dean crossed the kitchen in two long strides. When he reached her, she was pointing to the door of her office across the hall. The molding had been ripped from the frame, the lock forced, and with the door slightly ajar, he could glimpse one small section of the ransacked room.

"Somebody's trashed my office," Kate cried.

CHAPTER SIX

IGNORING THE broken pottery and spilled coffee at her feet, Kate stumbled toward the door of her office, her mind reeling with shock. Her favorite room, her refuge when her job and other pressures were too much to bear, had been desecrated. Destroyed. She shivered violently, feeling as if someone had attacked her own person.

Before she could enter the door, a strong hand grasped her arm and held her back.

"Don't go in there," Dean warned.

"I have to see what's missing." She swallowed a strangled sob. "What's ruined."

She tried to shake loose from his grip, but he held her tight. With masterful firmness mixed with tactful gentleness, he turned her around and led her back into the kitchen. Pulling out a chair at the table, he nudged her into it.

"Sit," he ordered. "I'll pour you another cup of coffee and then I'm calling the police. If you enter your office before they've investigated, you could destroy evidence that might lead them to the vandals."

He was right, of course, and she was shocked at how glad she was for his presence. He had been a rock of support when Mikey disappeared, and he was handling the break-in with a coolness and competence that amazed her. For a cowboy drifter, Dean Harding had a multitude of hidden strengths and talents. She'd never had a man to lean on, had always taken pride in her self-reliance, but this morning she welcomed the broad shoulders, the reassuring strength, and the cool reasoning he had offered without being asked.

Strange that bad things had begun happening only after he arrived.

She shoved the suspicious notion aside. Dean hadn't taken Mikey. He'd knocked himself out looking for her son. And as for her office—she recalled Dean coming onto the porch in the early morning hours and returning to his room before she had gone back to bed. Surely she would have heard him if he'd destroyed her private sanctuary? She refused to believe Dean could have been the vandal.

His deep, rich voice, confident and sure, filled the room as he related the relevant details to the 911 operator, and she found her frazzled nerves calming at the sound.

"Who would do such a thing?" she asked when he hung up the kitchen extension. Her hands shook with a mixture of rage and fear, and to hold them steady, she clenched them around the mug he'd handed her.

"You tell me." He sat across from her and fixed her with deep gray eyes that reminded her of summer thunderheads. "Were there valuables in the room?"

"Treasures. Family photos. Favorite books. My

most comfortable chair and a table that belonged to my great-grandmother. But nothing of any particular monetary value.''

He nodded, his eyes filled with understanding, and she bit her lower lip to fight back tears. Dollars and cents couldn't replace the keepsakes and memories that had been damaged, and she wouldn't know until the police arrived whether anything had been stolen.

"Stay here." He rose and strode out of the room, only to return a moment later. "Nothing's been touched in the parlor or dining room. Have you seen Mikey and your mother this morning? Are they okay?"

Warmed by his concern for her family, Kate nodded. "They were both sleeping when I came down for breakfast." Another fear struck her. "Did you check Felicity's room? It's closest to my office."

"I'm right as rain, Kate." The tall, white-haired woman, wrapped in a faded chenille bathrobe over her pajamas, stood on the threshold. "What's going on?"

"There's been a break-in in Kate's office," Dean explained.

"Heavenly days!" Felicity exclaimed. "And I slept through it? I could have been murdered in my bed!"

"Don't even think such a thing," Kate said with a shudder.

"Could you wake up the others?" Dean asked Felicity. "The police will be here any minute, and I'm sure they'll want to question everyone."

With a dignified nod, the older woman set her mouth in a grim line, cinched the sash on her robe tighter, and disappeared down the hallway.

Dean leaned against the kitchen counter, crossed his arms over his broad chest, and his boots at his ankles. His presence filled the room, an overpowering hulk of appealing masculinity whose quiet, easy manner seemed to hide a deeper, more serious personality. Secrets within secrets. That was the impression he gave, and Kate felt a sudden longing to reveal them all, to peel back the layers of Dean Harding until she could expose the true nature of the man inside.

"Did you lock the front door when you came inside early this morning?" he asked.

"Of course." She remembered clearly throwing the dead bolt before climbing the stairs to bed. After the scare of Mikey's disappearance, she'd become overly conscious of security.

Dean scowled. "I checked the front door. The lock wasn't forced, and that particular dead bolt is almost impossible to pick. Would have been easier to cut the glass door panels to get in, but they're unbroken."

She glanced toward the rear of the kitchen. "Maybe they came in through the back."

He shook his head. "Dead bolt and chain are both intact."

A possibility struck her and she gazed up at him, horrified. "You think someone has a key?"

His solemn eyes met hers without flinching. "At least seven people have keys to this house."

"No," she insisted. "It couldn't be one of the boarders. Why would any of them do such a thing?"

He shrugged. "Anger. Money. Revenge."

"Don't be ridiculous." His accusations annoyed her, taking her thoughts in a direction she didn't want to travel. How could she ever feel safe in her own home if she doubted the good intentions of the other residents? "Everyone here treats each other with respect and courtesy. Anger and revenge are definitely out."

"That leaves money."

"But there wasn't any money!"

He raised an eyebrow in an engaging expression. "Do the boarders know that?"

"No one goes in there but Mikey, Mom, and me. It's always locked." She studied him curiously. He seemed so adept at interrogation, she wondered if he'd done it before.

"So," he said in a reasonable tone, "someone might have broken in *expecting* to find money."

She shook her head. "Then why the destruction? What was done to my room was—" she searched for the right word "—hateful."

"If they didn't find the money they were anticipating, they might have taken out their anger through vandalism."

Kate propped her elbows on the table and buried her face in her hands. "I don't understand people who think—and act—that way."

In an instant, he was beside her, his large, gentle hands grasping her shoulders, turning her toward him.

His face was only inches from hers, and the generous width of his mouth, the closeness of his lips brought back memories of the delicious sensations of the kiss they'd shared.

She was losing her mind.

Her home had been violated, and she was fantasizing over a kiss. A meaningless kiss. A meaningless kiss that she couldn't get out of her mind, a meaningless kiss that had left her longing for more.

"Think hard, Kate," he insisted, his eyes so dark they were almost charcoal. "Has anyone been angry with you lately? Threatened you?"

Concentrating was hard with the warmth of his breath against her cheeks, his strong hands gripping her shoulders, his incredible eyes fastened on hers.

"No," she finally managed to mutter. "No one."

"You're positive?"

She was drowning in his eyes. How could she think with him so close that her pulse rate was fast approaching tachycardia? Wanting to slide into his arms and lean her head against the broad expanse of his chest, she forced herself to push away. She stood and carried her mug to the sink, emptied the tepid coffee, and rinsed the cup.

Away from his mesmerizing influence, her breath came easier, her thoughts cleared. "It's always possible I've angered or offended someone without being aware of it. Patients, for example."

"Which patients?" His question cracked through the room like a gunshot.

She pushed a strand of hair off her forehead and

turned to face him, her emotions under better control with the wide expanse of the kitchen table between them. "Some people expect doctors to work miracles. To be gods who solve all their problems. When a mother or a baby dies, to the survivors, it's the doctor's fault, no matter what caused the problem or how much effort went into saving the patient."

A strange look flickered across the handsome planes of Dean's face. Anger? Guilt?

Before she could analyze his expression, the door bell rang. His expression settled into more neutral lines. "That should be the police. Maybe they can sort this out."

Overwhelmed by her second crisis in less than two days, Kate followed him into the parlor, where the rest of the house's occupants were waiting.

BY TEN O'CLOCK that morning, after a drive of a little over an hour, Dean sat with William Garrett and Mitch Barnes in the great room of the Double G Ranch. From the loft area above them came the muted clicks of a keyboard, where Dylan was conducting a computer search on the backgrounds of the residents in Shelley Purvis's boardinghouse.

"Since there was no forced entry to the house itself," Dean said, "I figured it had to be an inside job—one of the residents with a key. Then Naomi Reddy admitted she had come home drunk from her opening-night party and probably forgot to lock the front door behind her."

"So it could have been anyone?" Mitch said.

Dean nodded grimly. "Could have been a cat burglar going from door to door in the neighborhood, looking for easy access."

William frowned. "But why hit Dr. Purvis's office and not the rest of the house?"

"It was the only room locked, so the thief could have assumed valuables were inside," Dean said with a shrug, but he didn't buy that theory. Something about the whole episode didn't sit right with him and had his rusty, but still viable, investigative instincts sounding alarm bells.

"What did the police find?" William was bouncing Hope, Mitch's baby daughter, on his knee, and the child squealed with laughter.

Dean couldn't help smiling at the baby. He had never spent much time with children, wasn't particularly comfortable with them, but Hope was especially appealing with her chubby cheeks, and Terry Monteverde's dark hair and almond-shaped eyes. He felt a stab of conscience that he was no closer to locating the girl's mother.

"Nothing missing," Dean replied, "but a lot of destruction. You could almost smell the viciousness in the air."

William glanced up from the baby. "Suspects?"

"None," Dean said. "The only prints in the room were Kate's, her mother's and Mikey's."

William smiled grimly. "Good thing you wore gloves when you explored it earlier, or you'd have a lot of explaining to do to the Austin police."

Dean turned to Mitch. "I'm sorry the search for

Terry is taking so long. Mikey's disappearance and this break-in have slowed down my investigation."

Mitch looked thoughtful. "Coincidence?"

William stopped jiggling Hope, set her on a blanket on the floor with her favorite Pooh bear, and frowned. "You think the break-in's related to Terry somehow?"

"Why not?" Worry creased Mitch's face. "Dean was looking for evidence of her whereabouts in Kate's office. Maybe somebody else had the same idea."

"But Leo Hayes is dead," William said. "The man who wanted her killed is no longer a threat to Terry. And we're positive he was working alone. Who else could be searching for her?"

"No one I can think of. And Kate...Dr. Purvis thinks the intruder could be a disgruntled patient," Dean said, "or a relative of one."

"That's always a possibility," Mitch said, "but if it's just coincidence, the doctor is having a hell of a string of bad luck. You've come to know her pretty well now, haven't you?"

Not well enough.

Dean recalled vividly the feel of her in his arms the night after Mikey had been found, remembered the honeyed taste of her mouth and the heady lilac scent of her. He knew her, all right, but not near as well as he wanted to.

And better than he should.

"What's your point?" he asked Mitch.

The former FBI agent leaned forward with his

hands clasped between his knees. "Tell her the truth, why you're really in Austin. Maybe then she'll tell you whether Hope is the baby she delivered that night and where we might find Terry."

Dean shook his head. "Not a chance. Kate Purvis is as by-the-book as they come. She won't breach doctor-patient privilege. I know her well enough to know that."

Dylan entered the great room, a single sheet of paper dangling between his fingers. "Every resident of the boardinghouse is clean—except one."

"Raoul?" Dean guessed. The police had already checked out Peter Tirrell after the incident with Mikey.

"Nope." A wide grin split Dylan's face. "Felicity Trent."

"Felicity has a police record?" Dean gaped in disbelief.

With a chuckle, Dylan handed Dean the sheet from his printer. "See for yourself. The woman was arrested for disorderly conduct in the sixties."

Dean scanned the paper and laughed.

"Share the joke," William demanded. "What's so danged funny?"

"The ever dignified and downright regal Felicity Trent," Dean explained, "burned her bra in a feminist demonstration in Atlanta."

William chuckled and shook his head. "Doesn't sound like she's our burglar."

"The burglar's the least of my worries. I've reached a dead end as far as finding Terry," Dean admitted, "until I can access the records at the hospital."

"I hope you find something there," Mitch said, "because I have another case I'd like you to work on as soon as you locate Terry."

Dean looked at Dylan, who kept him on retainer for Finders Keepers.

"Mitch has discussed it with me," Dylan said, "and I'd like you to take the case."

"Another missing person?" Dean asked.

Pain flooded Mitch's eyes. "My father."

"I'm sorry," Dean said. "How long's he been gone?"

Mitch scrunched his mouth in a crooked grin. "All my life. You see, I don't know who he is."

"Your mother?" Dean asked.

"Dead. And she never told me who my father was. From what she *did* say, I know he was either an itinerant cowboy from San Antonio or a traveling salesman from Kansas City. She loved the cowpoke, and when he left her, she found comfort in the arms of the salesman. Since she was never sure which man was my father, she refused to tell me more."

"Their names?" Dean asked.

Mitch shook his head. "Never could get her to say."

Dean let out a whistle. "I'm a good detective, but not that good. You want me to locate two unnamed men on a trail decades old?"

Mitch gazed at his daughter, curled asleep on the blanket with her stuffed toy in her arms. "I want

Hope to have family. If I can't find Terry, I'd like my daughter at least to know her grandfather. And I need to know for myself. The question's been haunting me my whole life."

"Give it a try, Dean," Dylan said. "If anyone can find him, you can."

Dean figured he had a snowball's chance in hell of locating Mitch's dad, but if Dylan and Mitch wanted him to try, he'd give it his best shot. He slid a small notebook and pen from the pocket of his chambray shirt. "Tell me about your mother."

"Her name was Bobby Jo Scott. She was a divorced waitress working in a Laredo honky-tonk when I was conceived. She took back her maiden name, Barnes, when I was born. In 1998, she died in a car accident." Mitch's tone turned wistful. "She never got to see her granddaughter."

On the other side of the room, William grew still, obviously moved by Mitch's story. Dean wasn't surprised at the older man's reaction. William Garrett's compassion was legendary.

"I'll see what I can find," Dean told Mitch, and shoved to his feet. "For now, I'd better hightail it back to Austin and figure out how to access the hospital records."

KATE TRUDGED up the front stairs of the boarding-house a little after noon. She'd reported for work at the hospital once the police had left that morning, but as soon as she'd completed her rounds, Abby sent her home.

"I'm fine," Kate had protested.

Abby shook her head. "You've been through two traumatic experiences back-to-back, plus the premature delivery. At least now you know the baby's condition's stable. Take time to get your room put together again or go for a walk, take in a movie. You'll be of more use to your patients if you're not a nervous wreck." The chief of staff grinned. "Besides, you've been a good girl. You deserve some time off, and I have enough people to cover for you this afternoon."

Not certain whether she was relieved or reluctant, Kate had headed home. Abby had been right about Kate's nerves being shot, but Kate had hoped work would take her mind off her problems. It would also keep her thoughts off Dean Harding, who seemed to have a monopoly on them lately.

When Kate arrived home, she tried to ignore the thrill of anticipation at the sight of Dean's pickup parked by the curb. Her willingness to indulge in a harmless flirtation with their newest boarder was effectively backfiring in her face. He'd been a rock of strength when Mikey disappeared, he'd kept her from going to pieces after last night's break-in, and she found herself longing to lean on him, to revel in his strength and quiet confidence.

Even worse, she *wanted* him.

She tried to convince herself she'd feel the same about any handsome man who lived in such close proximity. After all, she'd been a virtual celibate since Mikey had been born, avoiding both physical and emotional entanglements with the opposite sex, shutting herself off in her work. No wonder Dean Harding with his exceptional good looks and cowboy charm made her body ache with longing. She was a healthy female with normal instincts, and he had all the right equipment tied up in one heck of an attractive package.

Her lust, however, wasn't what frightened her. What scared her most was her desire for emotional connection, an irrefutable awareness that she wouldn't mind spending the rest of her life with such a man. A man she knew almost nothing about, except that he was good and kind and unselfish. And undeniably gorgeous. A man who could break her heart and stomp on the pieces, just like Steven had.

No, a harmless flirtation was no longer an option. Playing around with such an alluring man was playing with fire, and she'd already been badly burned once. She had the scar tissue to prove it. She couldn't—wouldn't—allow it to happen again.

With her emotions firmly reined in, she entered the house and headed for the kitchen in search of her mother. Her footsteps echoed in the empty downstairs rooms, and she found only Felicity, rolling out pastry on a granite countertop in the kitchen.

"Where's Mom?"

Startled, Felicity looked up, alarm spreading across her face. "What are you doing home? You're not ill?"

Kate shook her head. "I came home to straighten up the mess across the hall. Have you seen Mother and Mikey?"

"They went over to the Davidsons' so Mikey can play with Eric."

A flutter of anxiety kicked in beneath Kate's breast-bone. She hadn't yet recovered from the scare of Mikey's disappearance two nights earlier. "Was Mom going to leave him there?"

"Don't you worry, sweet pea. Shelley arranged with Mrs. Davidson for the boys to play in the back-yard, and your mother swore she wouldn't let him out of her sight." Felicity nodded toward the hallway. "We thought it was a good idea to keep Mikey out of the house while the crime scene unit was working. Hopefully, that mess will be cleaned up by the time he's home for supper."

Kate sagged into the nearest chair, overwhelmed at the prospect of repairing the destruction and restoring order to her sanctuary. Just the thought of her dev-astated room made her want to cry.

"It'll take forever just to clean away the fingerprint powder," Felicity said, "but Dean's making a good start."

"Dean?"

Mixed emotions assaulted her. Gratitude for Dean's willingness to help, reluctance to have the man in-vading her inner sanctum.

Felicity went to the refrigerator and removed a pitcher of tea and the makings for sandwiches. "You'll need some lunch before you tackle that job. Ham sandwich okay?"

"Yes, thanks," Kate replied absently, and wan-dered to the hall door. She saw no sign of Dean Harding in her study, but the battered door was missing from its hinges and the ruined molding gone.

She turned back to Felicity. "I thought you said Dean was working in there."

Felicity shook her head and pointed out the window over the sink. "He's out back."

Kate moved to the window, and her pulse jumped at the sight that confronted her. Dean, bare to the waist, his golden-tanned muscles slick with the sheen of perspiration, was bent over the study door, which he'd propped on sawhorses. Sunlight glinted off his hair, his fitted jeans hung low on narrow hips and his biceps rippled as he raked a carpenter's plane across the damaged wood, scraping away the splinters.

Kate was hungry all right, and he looked good enough to eat. She turned from the window with a groan. The prospect of keeping her distance from their handsome boarder had just become a whole lot less likely.

"I'm going upstairs to change clothes," she said. "I'll be right back."

"Kate?" Felicity looked up from her pie crust, rolling pin in one hand, flour dusting her right cheek. "Did you speak to Raoul today?"

"I haven't seen him, not since the police questioned us this morning."

"That's odd. He isn't here."

Kate cast a worried look at her elderly friend, fearing the emotional traumas of the past few days were taking a toll on Felicity's mind. "Of course, he's not," she said gently. "He's at work."

Felicity dusted flour off her hands and propped her fists on her hips. "Don't take me for an old fool, Kate. I know the man is usually at work at this time."

Kate shook her head in an attempt to clear the confusion. "What are you saying?"

"I went in a while ago to clean his room," Felicity explained. "All his things are gone."

"He's moved out?"

Felicity nodded. "Without a word to anyone. I find that strange, don't you? Especially right after your study was vandalized last night?"

Kate headed for her room on the third floor. Raoul's disappearance was strange all right, but it was just another in a series of strange happenings since Dean Harding had entered her life.

She hoped it was the last.

CHAPTER SEVEN

WITH THE SUN beating on his back, his muscles straining from the weight and movement of the electric sander, and perspiration dripping into his eyes, Dean was enjoying himself. The past few days he'd missed the physical exertion of working his ranch and had itched for the out-of-doors he'd become so accustomed to over the last few years.

The deep backyard of the boardinghouse didn't come close to the size of his own spread, but with its broad grassy lawn, tall shade trees, and flowering borders, it was a perfect spot to spend a summer afternoon. Bear, stretched out on her side beneath the nearest oak and whimpering as if she were chasing rabbits in her sleep, apparently agreed. Even so, Dean still missed his own home.

He'd found compensations at the boardinghouse, however. He'd been a loner most of his life, more so since his withdrawal to the ranch after Maggie's death, but he found to his surprise that he appreciated the company of the Purvises. He set aside the sander, grabbed a tack cloth, wiped the powdery sawdust from the study door, and considered the family he'd landed smack-dab in the middle of.

Kate's mother's unique individualism was a breath of fresh air, and he flourished under Shelley's maternal attitude. He'd been just a kid when his own mother died. His father had packed him off to live with a maiden aunt who always looked like she'd just tasted green persimmons. As a result, his boyhood hadn't been a happy one. Between Shelley and Felicity, however, he'd been almost mothered to death since coming to live at the boardinghouse, and he couldn't say he disliked it. Their warmth and concern helped fill a tiny bit of the hole Maggie's death had left in his heart.

And then there was Mikey.

Now there was a great kid. Dean and Maggie had talked about children, and Dean had longed for a son. Not that he hadn't wanted a daughter, but he'd particularly wanted a boy so he could give him all the love and nurturing Dean had missed growing up. If he and Maggie'd had a son, Dean mused, he'd want him to be just like Mikey, tough but affectionate, with an inquiring mind and a love of adventure.

At the slam of the screen door, he glanced toward the back porch. With the grace and elegance of a dancer and the exuberance of a teenager, Kate skipped down the back steps, a plate in one hand, a glass in the other. He set aside the tack cloth, wiped his hands on his jeans, and reached for his shirt, taking pleasure in watching her approach. Dressed in white shorts and a print top cropped at the waist, she crossed the lawn toward him, her slender hips swaying slightly, her long legs flashing the color of honey, and the sun shooting her hair full of golden highlights. He'd been thirsty before, but the sight of her made his mouth as dry as cotton.

"Hi," he said through parched lips. The heat accentuated the lilac scent of her, and it swirled around him, twisting him dizzy with desire.

"Hi, yourself." Her radiant smile made his insides quiver. "I brought you lunch."

He accepted the plate and tumbler she offered and guzzled half the glass of iced tea like a man dying of thirst. With his mouth wet, he found words easier. "Thanks. I'm not used to being waited on."

She shrugged and nodded toward the door he was repairing. "Just call it quid pro quo. Although lunch is mighty little to offer for such a big chore."

He couldn't resist the opening she'd given him. "Maybe you could add a little something."

Confusion clouded her remarkable brown eyes. "I don't understand."

"A little more quid for my quo?"

She swallowed hard and scanned the yard, as if willing to look anywhere but at him. "What kind of quid did you have in mind?"

He caught her gaze this time and held it. "What are you offering?"

A deep blush started at the top of her forehead and traveled to the open V of her blouse, where just a hint of delectable cleavage showed, and he knew they were thinking exactly the same thing, although he doubted she'd admit it.

"I—I could pay you," she stammered, looking like she wanted to run.

"I have a better idea." If he suggested the first thought that had entered his head, he'd get his face slapped. He settled for a safer option. "Have dinner with me tonight."

As if aware the conversation had just taken a less intimate turn, she relaxed and grinned. "I've had dinner with you the past several nights."

"That's true, but it's not what I meant. I'm a stranger here in Austin. I'd like to see some of the town. If I treat you to dinner at your favorite restaurant, maybe you can give me a tour."

She glanced at the door he'd finished repairing. "Sounds like a fair exchange. But you should let me buy dinner."

"No way—"

"But you don't have a job yet."

The intoxicating nearness of her had almost made him forget his undercover assignment. Kate didn't know that his Aunt Carrie, as if trying to compensate for the love she'd denied him in life, had left him a tidy sum in her will, enough to buy his ranch free and clear and have plenty left over for investments and entertainment.

"I have some good prospects for employment," he lied, "and enough to tide me over in the meantime."

She nodded. "I don't have a favorite restaurant, so you choose. What would you like? French, Thai, Japanese—"

"How about good old Texas-style barbecue?"

"There's a place in the hill country, and they have a band—" She broke off suddenly, seemingly flustered, as if she'd led herself in a direction she hadn't intended.

"How long since you went dancing, Kate?" he asked softly.

She shook her head. "I haven't danced since before I left Atlanta. I've probably forgotten how."

He grinned, happy at the prospect of holding her in his arms. "It's like riding a bicycle. It'll come back to you."

Tearing her gaze from his, she inclined her head toward the plate she'd brought him. "Better eat your sandwich before the bread dries out."

She turned to leave, but he caught her hand. "Stay with me."

Her flesh burned like fire against his skin, hotter than the Austin sun, but she didn't try to pull away. "There's work to do in my study—"

"I know. I'll help."

She cocked her head exactly as he'd seen Mikey do so often. "Why?"

He led her by the hand to a pair of Adirondack chairs beneath the live oak, where the temperature was about ten degrees cooler in the shade. She settled into one chair and he took the other, regretting that she'd loosened her hold on his hand. Curling one leg beneath her, she dangled the other, rubbing circles in the grass with the toe of her sandal. He couldn't help noticing the enticing pink polish adorning the nails of her very attractive toes. God help him, the woman was gorgeous all over—or at least as much of all over as he'd been able to see. At that thought, his temperature increased, in spite of the shade.

Bear, awakened by the odor of ham sandwich, ambled over to sit between them, confidently expectant of a tidbit, and Kate scratched the dog's ears.

"Why are you taking the time to help me," she repeated, "when you could be out looking for that job?"

He flashed his warmest smile and lied through his teeth. "I have an obsessive-compulsive personality. Can't stand clutter. Have to do something about it."

To keep himself from continuing to consider the parts of her he had yet to see, he took a huge bite of the ham sandwich and was amazed by the flavor that burst in his mouth. Being around Kate Purvis heightened his senses so that even his food tasted better.

For several minutes he munched contentedly, ignoring the small, still voice of his conscience reminding him that he was deceiving this woman, that if he ever wanted her to trust him, he was going about things all wrong. Thus far, his entire relationship with Kate had been built on lies, including the small one about his personality traits. But he couldn't confess now. He had a job to do. Only once he'd located the elusive Terry Monteverde would he be free to sort out his personal feelings.

"You're like Felicity," Kate observed. "A place for everything and everything in its place. I guess that's why Raoul's leaving has her so flustered."

The last bite of sandwich caught in his throat, and Dean swallowed hard. "Raoul left? When?"

Kate shrugged. "Sometime after the cops finished their interviews this morning. Didn't tell a soul. We wouldn't know he was gone if Felicity hadn't started to clean his room and realized all his belongings are missing."

Warning bells clanged in Dean's brain. "Raoul Davega is from South America, right?"

Kate scrunched her nose in a delightful expression, as if trying to remember. A sudden light glimmered in her eyes. "Brazil. Rio de Janeiro."

Bingo.

Rio, where Terry Monteverde had operated her family's gem business. Maybe William and Dylan were wrong and Leo Hayes *did* have a partner, someone who was still on Terry's trail, just like Dean was.

Dean stood and began buttoning his shirt. "Do you know where Raoul works?"

Kate crooked her neck and stared up at him. "Triple-Z Air-Conditioning. Why?"

"We don't really know why Raoul left or if he's okay. He's all alone in this country." He was embarrassed at how quickly the lies came to him. "Don't you think somebody ought to check on him? Make sure he's all right?"

Looking sheepish, Kate pushed to her feet. "I should have thought of that. If I hadn't been so self-absorbed with the break-in, I would have. I'll show you where the Triple-Z plant is, if you want to go there."

Tucking in his shirt, Dean struggled to hide his own discomfort. His reasons for checking out Raoul's disappearance were far from charitable. He suspected the former boarder might have been the culprit who'd broken into Kate's office—why else would he have taken off without notice?—but Dean couldn't share his suspicions with her without blowing his cover.

"How far is the plant from here?" he asked.

"About a fifteen-minute drive. I'll get my sunglasses and meet you out front."

TWO HOURS LATER, Dean and Kate were back at the boardinghouse, where Dean had rehung the repaired door and mended the broken table with wood glue. Sitting atop a ladder, he replaced books on the top shelf of the bookcase as Kate handed them to him. Felicity had retreated to her room for a short nap after removing the last of the fingerprint powder from the room's surfaces.

Kate picked up a book, dusted it with a cloth, then stood staring at it as if her thoughts were a thousand miles away.

"You okay?" Dean asked.

Not for the first time since they'd returned to her study did he have to resist the urge to gather her in his arms. He could tell the destruction of her study depressed her, but he'd hoped her spirits would improve once they'd cleared up the mess and repaired the damage. He had yet, however, to observe her perking up.

She handed him the book. "I'm concerned about Raoul."

"He's a smart young man. I'm sure he can take care of himself."

She leaned on the stepladder, crossed her arms on a rung, and stared up at him with worried eyes. "It doesn't make sense for him to leave without telling us. Or without telling his boss, either."

At the air-conditioning company, Raoul's boss had informed them Raoul had received a phone call as soon as he arrived at work that morning. The next thing his boss knew, Raoul was gone, without collecting the pay that was owed him. He hadn't reported in, hadn't left a message, hadn't told any of his co-workers where he was going or why. That highly suspicious conduct had Dean spinning all sorts of ominous theories, but none he could share with Kate.

"People do funny things," he said, hoping to ease her fears for the former boarder. "When I was in high school, my best friend's mother disappeared for three days. Her family was frantic. On the fourth day, she showed up at home as if nothing had happened."

"Had she lost her memory?"

Dean grinned. "Nope. But with a husband who was seldom home and three active teenagers, she was afraid she was losing her mind. She took what she called a mental health weekend."

"You're kidding."

He shook his head. "She checked into a local hotel with a bucket of Kentucky Fried Chicken and a bottle of Wild Turkey. When she'd watched all the movies on cable and the food and booze had run out, she went home, prepared to face her hectic life again.''

''What did her family say?''

''They were so happy she was alive and well, they weren't angry. And everyone pitched in after that to help out more around the house. They were a great family. I loved to spend time with them.'' He couldn't keep the wistfulness from his voice.

Kate dusted another book and handed it to him. ''What about your family?''

He shrugged. ''Didn't really have one. My mother died when I was in elementary school—not much older than Mikey is now. My dad was an airline pilot, so my aunt Carrie raised me. She was a real piece of work.''

Kate smiled. ''Like my mom?''

The image of his aunt being anything like Shelley Purvis made him laugh. ''Your mother enjoys life to the fullest. That's a trait Aunt Carrie never developed. She was the original doom-and-gloom queen. Always expecting the worst and usually getting it. If I made the football team, she figured I'd die from a concussion. If my grades were good, that meant they could only go down next time. If the sun shone, rain had to be on the way. You get the idea.''

Kate shuddered with sympathy. ''Not a very happy atmosphere for a little boy.''

''Aunt Carrie wasn't a happy person. She viewed everything in life as either sinful, dangerous or likely to get your clothes dirty. She was the travel agent for guilt trips. Nothing I did pleased her.''

He stopped, embarrassed to have shared so much. He'd never talked about Aunt Carrie to anyone before, not even Maggie. For years, he'd kept his bitterness and unhappiness about his childhood locked inside. Maybe he'd shared his feelings with Kate because, having Mikey, she'd understand what life had been like for Dean as a little boy.

Or maybe he'd told her just because she was Kate.

With a start, he realized he was falling in love with Dr. Kate Purvis. Not that it would do him any good. Once she discovered how he'd deceived her, she'd never want to see him again, much less return his feelings. Resigned to losing the best thing that had happened to him since Maggie, he took the book Kate handed him and placed it on the shelf.

He'd better enjoy his evening out with her tonight. It would probably be the only one he'd ever have.

IN A SECLUDED BOOTH at the restaurant, Kate had to make a conscious effort to keep from enjoying herself too much. Being there with Dean Harding wasn't a date, she reminded herself, just payback for the repairs he had done on her study. She'd already reached the conclusion he was too hot to handle for a harmless flirtation, and if she didn't want her heart broken again, polite but distant was her best move.

The evening had started a few hours earlier when they'd left Mikey with Shelley in the parlor of the boardinghouse. Watching a Disney video with his grandmother, the boy had munched happily on popcorn, slipping the fluffy kernels every few minutes to a very contented Bear curled at his feet. Bear was another complication Dean had brought into her life. Mikey adored that dog and would be heartbroken when Dean left and took Bear with him. Then Shelley would insist on Mikey having a puppy, and Kate wouldn't have the heart to refuse.

Damn the man. He'd turned her entire peaceful life upside down. Biggest problem was, she *liked* it.

In the extended daylight hours of the summer evening, Kate had taken Dean on a whirlwind tour of Austin. She had shown him the State Capitol Building, the Governor's Mansion, and the campus of the University of Texas. They had even walked the length of the Drag, the locals' name for the Twenty-Third Street Renaissance Market on Guadalupe, where artisans sold handmade items, everything from hemp jewelry to wind chimes.

Kate soon became acutely aware that Dean's attention wasn't on sightseeing. She'd be pointing out a local landmark and explaining its significance, only to find his gaze focused on her instead. Once, outside the Governor's Mansion, his intense scrutiny had caused her to lose her train of thought and stumble over her words as she explained that the governor and his family lived in a private suite on the second floor.

"Am I boring you?" she asked defensively.

His eyes, a soft silky gray that she could lose herself in, shimmered with interest. "I've never been less bored in my life."

"I know I sound like a tour guide—"

"You're giving me exactly what I want." His deep rich voice was thick with innuendo.

"A tour of the sights of Austin?"

He nodded. "I've seen the best Austin has to offer."

He wasn't talking about the buildings. She'd have to be deaf and blind not to get his drift. His slow, easy grin made kamikaze butterflies dive bomb in her stomach, ratcheted her pulse up an extra twenty beats per minute, and doubled her respiration rate.

"Hungry?" she asked, hoping to change the intense direction of the conversation.

"Starving." His eyes devoured her.

Suddenly filled with a craving herself, she'd avoided his gaze, not wanting to admit that the yearning she'd seen there mirrored her own. She couldn't invest in a relationship that obviously had no future. What did she, a physician, have in common with a cowboy drifter besides desire?

That's a good start, her heart taunted.

A dangerous start, her head replied.

She could have resisted him better if she hadn't been experiencing that deep hunger at this very moment, an itch that longed to be scratched.

Go home now, her head warned. *Put as much physical and emotional distance between yourself and this alluring man as possible.*

Shut up, her heart responded. *Dean Harding might be the best thing that's happened to you since Mikey was born. Don't blow this chance.*

As if oblivious to her head and heart, her traitorous

body simply yearned for more. More of his company. More of everything.

Besides, she argued with herself, she *had* promised him dinner for his troubles, and backing out on her offer wouldn't be polite. She was a big girl who should have no problem keeping her impulses under control for just one evening.

Right, her intellect reminded her. *Last time you said that you ended up pregnant.*

But she was older and wiser now, and should be able to handle dinner with a handsome man without going off the deep end. At least, that's what she'd told herself.

In the hill country northwest of Austin, she leaned back in the dimly lighted booth of the restaurant with its roadhouse decor, the best barbecue she'd ever tasted, and a live country-and-western band. Now that they'd eaten, there was no reason to linger.

Except for the attractive man seated across from her.

His long fingers drummed lightly on the table in time with the catchy tune to which several of the other customers were line dancing. Even in scant illumination, she could read the light in his eyes.

"This is a great place," Dean said. "You come here often?"

"Actually, this is my first time. A friend at work told me about it."

"You don't get out much, do you?"

She bristled at the sympathy in his voice. "As much as I like."

The sharpness of her voice didn't deter him. "If you don't come here, where do you go?"

She couldn't fault the friendly interest in his tone and forced herself to relax. He was just making conversation, after all, and where was the harm in that? "Mostly places where I can take Mikey."

"And is Mikey the only man in your life?"

"For now." His question annoyed her, but whether because it was too personal or too true, she couldn't tell. She decided to fight fire with fire. "What about you? You move around a lot. Do you have a woman in every town?"

He grew suddenly quiet, and she wished she could snatch the question back. He took a sip of his beer and wiped condensation from the glass mug with his fingertip. "My wife died from cancer almost six years ago. There's been no one since."

His answer shocked her. She had never figured Dean Harding for the marrying type, but from the depth of the sorrow etched on his handsome face, she could tell he'd loved his wife deeply and still mourned her death.

"I'm sorry," she said. "That must have been hard for you."

"It almost killed me." He spoke so softly she had to strain to hear the words.

She reached across the table and placed her hand over his. His skin was comfortingly warm and he turned his palm upright and twined his fingers with hers.

"But life goes on," he said, as if shaking off bad

memories. "It's taken me a while, but I've learned that. Have you?"

She tried to withdraw her hand, but he held it tight. "What do you mean?"

"Sounds to me like you've buried yourself in work since Mikey's father walked out on you. That's not living. That's merely existing."

Anger fired within her. "How dare—"

"Because I've been there. I know what it's like to lose someone, something precious. You want to crawl in a hole, pull the dirt over your head, and make the world go away. Look at yourself. You work long hours. What time you don't spend at work, you spend with your son. How long since you did something just for Kate?"

His words hit home, and she countered with more anger. "What about you? How long since you did something just for Dean?"

"Too damned long. That's why I'm here tonight. Dance with me."

The band had switched from a foot-stomping rhythm to a slow, easy tune. Couples clung together, barely moving, on the dance floor.

Dubious, she shook her head. "I don't—"

"Dammit, Kate, I'm not asking for a lifetime commitment. Just one dance."

When he put it that way, it seemed foolish to refuse. But the minute she stepped onto the dance floor and he slid his arms around her, she knew she'd made a mistake, headed in a direction she couldn't step back from. Her body melded to his as if they'd originally been one piece, broken apart only to find each other again. Dizzy with passion, she couldn't tell where she ended and he began as she melted into the encompassing warmth of his embrace.

One dance segued into another, but they didn't leave the floor. She could feel his lips upon her hair, hear the thud of his heart beneath her cheek as their bodies swayed to the sensuous rhythm of the music. He'd said he wasn't asking for commitment, just a dance, but she hadn't felt so cherished, so safe, so incredibly alive since before Mikey was born. Even if the experience was only for tonight, she needed to *feel* again, to acknowledge what she'd been missing all those long, lonely years.

What she'd miss again when the transient cowboy moved on.

Dean didn't speak while they danced, but words weren't necessary. She felt connected to him in a way she'd never experienced with Steven. Just being close to the strong, silent cowboy was enough. Conversation was superfluous.

When the music stopped and Dean released her, she noted with surprise that the band was packing up its instruments. The dream had ended, and reality crashed in on her again.

"It's two o'clock," Dean said. "Closing time."

She groaned. "I've got rounds in four hours."

"Then I'd better take you home to bed."

She struggled against the desire his words aroused. Thank heavens, they both lived at the boardinghouse. Kate couldn't sleep with Dean without Shelley's knowledge—not that her mother would disapprove. But bringing her mother and Mikey into the equation helped put Kate's emotions back on an even keel. She could see no future for herself and the cowboy, and the deeper she became entangled with him, the more hurt they'd both suffer when they parted.

Sharply aware of his hand on her elbow, she walked with him to her car. The cold night air helped clear her mind, and by the time they reached the front porch of the boardinghouse, her resolution to keep her distance had returned. She unlocked the front door, and Dean followed her inside, switching off the porch light as he locked the front door behind him.

"Thanks." She retreated a few steps down the hall. "I had a great time."

He followed, took her hand with one of his and flipped off the foyer lights with the other. Moonlight streamed in the beveled glass of the front door, and she could still see his face clearly, even in the gloom. Desire glistened in his eyes and pulsed in the vein at his neck. He pulled her toward him.

She placed her palm against the hard expanse of his chest and backed against the wall of the hallway. "This isn't a good idea."

The heat in his smile almost undid her. "It's the best idea I've had all night."

"But I'm afraid—"

"Afraid of kissing me?"

"Afraid of where that kiss might lead."

"We won't go anywhere you don't want to." His

breath brushed her cheek, sending delicious shivers down her spine.

"You don't understand." She was having trouble breathing and could hardly speak.

He tugged her closer until her body molded to his. "Then maybe you'd better explain."

"I can't."

"Can't explain?"

"Can't get involved."

He positioned a hand on the wall on either side of her, fencing her in. "I didn't know chastity was part of the Hippocratic Oath."

"It isn't."

"Good." He lowered his lips to hers, apparently finished with talking and ready for action.

She placed her hands on his chest to push him away, but found instead that her fingers twined in his shirt, pulling him closer as her mouth opened to his. Desire weakened her knees, and she was glad for the support of the wall against her back and the hard, full-length pressure of Dean's body against hers, igniting every nerve ending with longing.

He slid his arms around her, cupping her backside, lifting her to her toes. Her breasts, crushed against his chest, burned like wildfire. She dug her fingers into his hair and moaned softly as his tongue danced with hers.

He skimmed his hands up her body beneath her blouse. His touch scorched the skin of her back as his fingers kneaded her muscles, sending exquisite ripples of pleasure straight to her core. She arched against him with a soft cry.

He murmured her name as he kissed the length of her throat, buried his face in the opening of her blouse. Her breasts ached for his touch. Another minute and she'd be ripping off his clothes—and her own. Digging deep for her last ounce of self-restraint, she managed to break free.

"Bad idea," she murmured, gasping for air.

He cocked his head and smiled with an appeal that almost broke her resolve again. "I thought you were enjoying it."

"Oh, I was," she said with more feeling than she'd intended. She headed for the stairs and grasped the newel post to keep her unstable legs from giving out on her. "Which is exactly why it was a bad idea."

"Kate."

She should have kept going, marched right up the stairs to her room, but the deep timbre of his voice calling her name grabbed her as surely as if he'd lassoed and hog-tied her. She turned to face him again.

The moonlight outlined his powerful physique in the darkness of the hallway. "I just wanted to thank you for the best evening I've had in years."

She was glad he hadn't moved toward her again. If he had, she couldn't have resisted throwing herself in his arms, begging to be kissed again. Begging him to take her to his room, to his bed. Events were moving too fast, and her emotions were too frazzled for her to think straight.

"You're welcome," she managed to say between

lips still trembling from his kiss. "I had a good time, too."

As if the devil were on her heels, she raced upstairs to the safety of her room.

CHAPTER EIGHT

WITH BEAR CURLED against his side, Dean lay awake long after he'd gone to bed. He couldn't get Kate Purvis out of his mind, and it was his own damned fault. The scent of her still teased his nostrils, his hands longed to hold her, and his entire body ached with desire. He should have left her alone, done his job, and disappeared. But he hadn't been able to resist her—her warmth, her beauty, her compassion. He'd never known a woman like her and was well aware he wasn't likely to meet her match ever again.

Not that he hadn't loved Maggie.

Mags had been special—would always be special, his very first love. But they'd been kids when they'd met and married, and they'd only had a few years to grow up before the specter of cancer hung over them and darkened the rest of their days together.

Without taking anything away from his love for his wife, he could freely admit he'd never felt the passion for a woman that Kate Purvis generated in him.

Not that those feelings would do him a hill of beans worth of good.

If everything worked out, in less than forty-eight hours he'd be headed back to the Garretts with the information on Terry Monteverde and then home to his ranch. All he'd have left of Kate Purvis would be the memory of that kiss. She'd wanted him, all right. Wanted him as badly as he'd wanted her, but Dean wasn't the love-'em-and-leave-'em type. Sex with a woman like Kate meant commitment, and how could he commit to a woman he'd consistently lied to from the first moment they'd met?

Under other circumstances, he could return to Austin after his case was ended, but not these. Kate wasn't the kind of woman who'd take lightly to lies, who'd be willing to forgive and forget his deception. After the way her father and Steven had treated her, she'd made it clear she'd lost patience with men who let her down.

Rolling over, he punched the pillow beneath his head, searching in vain for comfort and peace of mind. He'd have to be satisfied with tonight's kiss, then try to put the beautiful doctor out of his mind.

Forget Kate? Fat chance.

With a groan, he attempted to sleep, but blissful unconsciousness eluded him. As if aware of his restlessness, Bear moved closer and rested her chin against his chest. With a frustrated sigh, he stroked the fur on her back. Why couldn't the love between a man and a woman be as uncomplicated as his relationship with his dog? Bear loved him without question and without conditions. She'd defend him to the death and never leave him, no matter how many lies he told her. Much as he loved his dog, however, her unqualified affection was little compensation for the longing he felt for the woman sleeping right above his head, as unattainable as if she lived on the far side of the moon.

Dean tossed and turned for hours, striving in vain for sleep and trying just as futilely to convince himself he could forget Kate Purvis once this case was finished. At five o'clock, he heard her soft footsteps pass his door, and he drew on every bit of self-restraint to keep from throwing on his clothes and joining her in the kitchen.

Against his better judgment, he'd given in to his feelings for her last night, acted on them, and made her aware of how he felt. The kindest thing he could do now was to see as little as possible of her before he disappeared for good. He lay in bed, picturing her moving efficiently around the kitchen, making coffee, having her usual yogurt and English muffin before rushing off to her morning rounds. He visualized those clear brown eyes, still a little puffy from sleep, the porcelain beauty of her complexion, the sleek perfection of her hair, the soft curves of her body beneath her sensible work clothes, her lips still swollen and bruised from his kiss....

With a groan, he covered his head with his pillow and mentally counted the posts on the fence that rimmed the acreage of his ranch until his breathing slowed and he dropped into blessed sleep.

SEVERAL HOURS LATER, Dean fought the Austin traffic and turned his truck onto Mayfair Avenue in the heart of Austin. If he was going to break into the hospital records room that night, he had to do some reconnoitering first.

He slowed the pickup as he approached Maitland Maternity Clinic and pulled into the sweeping drive that led to the front entrance. Following the drive around the corner, he parked beneath the shade of a cottonwood at the edge of the spacious but already crowded lot. He spotted Kate's car in the space reserved with her name and reminded himself he'd have to be careful not to run into her while he did his snooping. Rolling down both windows to ensure a breeze for Bear, he instructed the dog to remain in the truck.

Avoiding the double doors at the back entrance, which seemed to handle most of the hospital's traffic, he circled the building to the front doors and strolled inside. Only one security guard was visible. Dean assumed there was at least one other, probably standing guard at the rear entrance. Several people sat in the waiting room, decorated in soothing pastel colors. He approached a directory posted on the lobby wall and scanned it carefully. The records room and Kate's office were both located on the second floor.

He did a quick reconnaissance of the first floor, noting the small gift shop, a coffee shop, several other offices and a daycare center. Signs indicated the labor and delivery rooms were also located on this floor, and he remained poised for Kate's unexpected appearance. If she spotted him, he'd have to lie to her again and say he'd come to ask her to lunch. Fortunately, although he saw several other doctors, some in green scrubs, others in white lab coats, he never ran into Kate.

Making a mental map of the elevators and stairs to the second floor, Dean decided he didn't dare risk meeting Kate by going upstairs while she was on duty. He satisfied himself that with so many visitors and staff bustling through the clinic, he was unlikely to draw much attention when he returned later today if he simply moved with purpose.

Mission accomplished, he returned to his truck to find Bear snoozing on the shaded seat. She sprang to life as the door opened, woofed happily at the sight of him, and wagged her tail. Her loyalty was a balm to his spirit. If Bear loved him, he couldn't be all bad, in spite of the way he'd deluded Kate Purvis.

IN THE DOCTORS' locker room, Kate tossed her bloodied scrubs into the laundry basket. Her last delivery had been routine, an eight-pound, seven-ounce boy with mother and baby both in excellent health. She was buttoning her blouse when Abby popped in.

"You okay?" her friend asked.

"Sure. Why?"

"Scarrett said you seemed distracted during this morning's delivery."

Scarrett, head nurse of the delivery room, was the Maitland Maternity equivalent of an Army drill sergeant. Her sharp eyes missed nothing, and anything she considered off-kilter, she reported directly to Abby, her CO.

"Didn't get much sleep last night." Kate winced

at the lie. She hadn't slept at all. Once she'd gone to bed, all she could think of was Dean Harding, lying in the single bed, alone, below her on the second floor, and how much she longed to descend the stairs, crawl in alongside him, and finish what they'd started in the hallway. The sound of her alarm had been a blessing, ending hours of torment.

"Everything okay at home?" Abby asked.

"Yes...no."

"I'm listening."

"Mom and Mikey are fine...."

"But?"

"I'm a basket case."

"Has to be a man."

Kate's eyes widened in surprise. "What makes you think so?"

"I've never known anything else to rattle you, except when Mikey went missing. You've got a reputation for remaining cool and collected, especially in a crisis. I figure this morning's distraction has to be the cowboy."

Kate narrowed her eyes. "That's more than a lucky guess."

Abby shrugged. "Okay, so I called last night to see how the cleanup on your office was progressing. Shelley told me you'd gone to dinner with your star boarder."

"That's my mom. I'm surprised she didn't lease airtime on the local stations so everyone in Austin would know."

"You're angry. The evening didn't go well?"

Kate slumped onto a bench and leaned against a locker. "It went well, all right. Too well."

"But that's good."

Kate shook her head.

"Why not?"

"I think I'm falling in love with him."

"What's wrong with love?"

"Nothing, if it leads somewhere. I'm afraid this is another dead-end relationship."

"Like Steven? You can't judge every man by your one mistake."

"It's more than that. Dean doesn't have a job, he's secretive about his background, and I get the distinct impression he's just marking time, waiting to move on."

"Have you talked to him about his plans?"

Remembering, Kate blushed. "We didn't do much talking."

"Ahhh."

"It's not what you think. I didn't sleep with him, although, Lord knows, I wanted to badly enough."

"Regrets?"

Kate shook her head. "I know I did the right thing, but I hate it."

Abby settled on the bench beside her. "Maybe you're selling your cowboy short. Shelley told me he spent most of yesterday repairing the damage to your study. A man that thoughtful can't be all bad."

"You could be right—"

"I often am," Abby said with a grin.

"I'm afraid to take the risk," Kate admitted.

"Love is *always* a risk. You're a doctor. You know how ephemeral life is, even when love is strong."

Kate remembered the pain on Dean's face when he'd spoken of his wife's death. He'd also spoken of life going on. Had she put her life on hold after Steven's treachery? Was she letting the unfaithfulness of one man keep her from loving again? Or were the subtle signals of trouble she had picked up from Dean Harding real?

She groaned and ran her fingers through her hair. "I don't know what to do."

Abby stood and placed her hand on Kate's shoulder with a friendly squeeze. "Maybe you should just let nature take its course."

"Lord, no," Kate laughed. "This hospital is a monument to where that leads."

"Then the next best thing is chocolate. They're serving chocolate-covered doughnuts in the coffee shop this morning."

Kate stood and straightened her skirt. "Now that's a prescription I can follow."

AN HOUR LATER, Kate climbed the front steps of the porch to find her mother ensconced in a wicker rocker, shelling peas while listening to talk radio on her tiny portable.

"What are you doing home?" Shelley asked in surprise.

Kate swooped down on her mother with a hearty hug and kiss. "Just decided to come home for lunch. Where's Mikey?"

"He went to the grocery store with Felicity. But Dean is in the kitchen having a late breakfast."

Kate straightened in surprise. "What makes you think—"

"I'm not so old I don't recognize budding love when I see it."

Sinking into the chair beside her mother's, Kate shook her head. "I hadn't figured it out for myself until just a few minutes ago. How did you know?"

Her mother blessed her with a loving smile. "I saw the spark in your eyes the first day Dean Harding set foot in this place. Took you long enough to realize it."

"After Dad and Steven, I was afraid."

Shelley's forehead wrinkled with worry. "And now you're not?"

Kate shook her head. "I've decided if I let fear hold me back, I could miss out on the best things in life. I'm better off taking chances, not missing what comes along."

"Have you told Dean how you feel?"

"That's why I came home. And I thought I'd ask him to go to the outdoor concert with us tonight."

"Mikey will like that. So will I."

Kate stood and kissed her mother on the cheek. "Thanks for understanding."

Her mother reached out and squeezed her hand. "That's what moms are for."

With anticipation fluttering beneath her breastbone, Kate entered the house and headed for the kitchen. She found Dean sitting at the big table, looking as if he hadn't slept well. Suddenly awkward, she hesitated in the doorway. "Hi."

When he saw her, he jumped to his feet. "Is something wrong?"

"No. I came home to have lunch with you."

A flurry of reactions skidded across his handsome features, too fast for her to read. "Mind telling me why?"

Her breath caught in her throat. She could face the issue head-on now, or she could skirt it again, just as she'd been doing since they first met. She straightened her shoulders and decided to go for it. "Because being with you makes me happy. Because I'm sorry last night ended the way it did."

He crossed the room in three strides and gripped her by the shoulders, his eyes filled with emotion that seemed to shift between love and pain. "You don't even know me, Kate. I—"

She pressed her fingers against his lips. "I know all I need to know. You're gentle, kind, considerate. And you make me feel like a woman again."

With unaccustomed boldness, she lifted her arms around his neck and raised her lips to his. At first, she feared she'd made a terrible mistake, because he didn't respond. Then his arms flew around her, tightening until she almost couldn't breathe and lifting her off her feet. His lips claimed hers with the passion she remembered from the night before.

He loves me, she thought with satisfaction, her fears melting beneath the heat of his kiss. *Everything's going to be all right.*

With obvious regret, Dean pulled away. "You won't have time to eat if we keep this up."

Leaning her head against his chest, her arms around his waist, she felt like purring with happiness. "Who needs food?"

"You do. You didn't get much sleep last night, and you need energy from somewhere or you won't make it through the rest of the day." He led her to a chair and forced her gently into it. "Let me make you something."

With fascination, she watched him assemble a sandwich and pour her a glass of tea. Now that she'd thrust her fears aside and admitted to herself how much she cared for this man, she found herself intrigued with his every movement, delighted with each nuance of expression that crossed his face. She felt she could spend two lifetimes with him and never grow bored.

"You're not eating," he reprimanded.

She took a bite of the sandwich, chewed and swallowed. "There's an outdoor concert tonight. Would you like to come with Mom, Mikey and me?"

He took the chair across from her, regret etching the handsome features of his face. "I can't."

"Oh." Disappointment welled in her, sharper than she could have imagined.

"I'd like to," he said with a sincerity she didn't doubt, "but I have an invitation to dinner with a prospective employer. I don't know what time we'll be through."

She forced a smile, reminding herself that he

needed the work. "A prospect. That's good. What kind of job?"

His slow grin warmed her to her toes. "I'll tell you afterward. Don't want to jinx it by saying too much beforehand."

Content just to be in his company, she finished her sandwich, then glanced at her watch. "Oh, my gosh, I have to get back. Maybe I can see you after the concert?"

"It's a date." He walked her to the door of the kitchen and kissed her lightly on her lips. "Sorry about the concert."

"No problem," she said. "There'll be others."

She rushed to her car on feet that didn't seem to touch the ground, unaware that Dean watched her go, his face darkened with a frown.

BY THE TIME Dean returned to the hospital at six o'clock that evening, he'd had a full day, and he'd been glad for the activities that kept his mind off Kate. Their relationship had gone further than he'd intended, and he didn't know how to slow things down. Their attraction to each other was like an unstoppable juggernaut, a runaway train, and possibly even a disaster waiting to happen.

After lunch, he'd made the hour-plus trip to the Double G to fill in Dylan and William on Raoul Davega's mysterious disappearance. While Dean talked with William on the broad front veranda, Dylan had made phone calls to some of his contacts.

"You seem worried," William observed as Dean settled in a rough-barked chair beside him.

Dean thought immediately of Kate Purvis, but he hesitated to mention his dilemma to William. He couldn't lie to the man either, so he sidestepped the issue. "I'm fine."

"I thought maybe you were anxious to get back to your ranch."

"I was."

Dean smothered a sigh. At first, all he'd wanted was to return to his ranch, where the ever present solitude had been a balm to his grieving soul. Since living among the lively residents of the boarding-house, however, his ranch loomed as a lonely and forbidding place.

"There's plenty of work waiting for me there," Dean admitted, again avoiding expressing his true thoughts. "How are things on the Double G?"

Apparently aware that Dean didn't want to talk about his personal feelings, William tactfully turned the conversation to the business of running his own ranch. Chatting with William about the Double G helped Dean push Kate from his mind for a little while.

In less than a half hour, Dylan joined them again. "My contacts at the airlines say Raoul Davega flew out of Austin at noon yesterday, bound for Rio."

William scratched his head and scowled. "It can't be a coincidence the man's from the same city as Terry Monteverde."

"Or that he disappears the morning after Kate

Purvis's home office was vandalized," Dean observed. "Chances are good the two events are connected somehow."

"What are the odds," Dylan asked, "that you missed something when you searched the doctor's study? Any chance Raoul found evidence there that Terry has returned to Brazil?"

"No way," Dean stated with absolute certainty. "Kate kept no records from her work at home."

"I've contacted a private investigator in Rio," Dylan said. "He's going to check out Davega from that end."

"So what will you do now?" William asked Dean.

"I'll check the hospital records tonight and hope they can lead us to Terry."

"Then you'll be leaving Austin?" Dylan asked.

Dean nodded, hiding the sorrow that stabbed him at the prospect. "Unless I discover that's where Terry's hiding."

SITTING IN HIS pickup in the shade of the same cottonwood where he'd parked earlier that day, Dean found himself regretting his imminent departure from the boardinghouse. He'd miss the mothering Shelley and Felicity had provided, and Mikey's boyish rambunctiousness, but most of all, he'd miss everything about Kate Purvis.

With a sigh, he opened the door and stepped from his truck. Pining for Kate was a lost cause. She'd never forgive him for deceiving her. Once he'd found

information on Terry Monteverde's whereabouts, he
had no choice but to move on.

He thought wistfully of Kate, Mikey and Shelley,
finishing dinner now at the boardinghouse before
leaving for the outdoor concert on the banks of Lake
Austin. He'd have the entire supper hour and the
length of the concert to conduct his search in the hospital without worrying about running into Kate.

With his lock-picking kit tucked in the pocket of
his jeans, Dean reached into the toolbox in the bed
of his truck and removed a harness for Bear, the type
used by the visually handicapped for their guide dogs.
Since she'd worn this disguise before, Bear stood patiently while Dean attached it. Sliding on the dark
glasses he'd taken from his pocket, he grasped the
harness handle and headed for the less busy front entrance of the hospital.

The bustle of people he'd noted that morning had
diminished. Fewer occupied the waiting room, although the coffee shop was doing a brisk business
with visitors and staff picking up a quick sandwich
for supper. Passing the security guard without a hitch,
Dean strode to the elevator with Bear at his side. Only
guide or companion dogs were allowed in hospitals,
and Dean needed Bear to stand watch while he con-
ducted his search.

He stepped off the elevator into an empty second-
floor corridor. To his left, a sign indicated the records
room. To his right was Kate's office. He decided to
try the records room first and hoped it was staffed
only during regular office hours. From his earlier

phone inquiries, he was certain that a hospital employee would refuse to answer his questions. He knocked at the solid door. When no one appeared, he slipped on latex gloves. When he twisted the doorknob, he wasn't surprised to find the door locked.

"Keep your ears open, Bear. If you hear anyone coming, let me know."

Bear woofed softly in acknowledgement.

With the tools from his kit, he quickly picked the lock, opened the door, and relocked it behind him when he and Bear were inside. In the early summer evening, sunshine from a row of windows flooded the room, so he didn't need to turn on any lights that might attract unwanted attention.

"Stay here." He motioned to the door, and Bear sat obediently. "Let me know if someone's coming."

Bear wagged her tail. With her acute sense of hearing, she made a better watchman than any human accomplice.

Dean hurried to a wall filled with lateral files. He searched first under Monteverde, but found nothing. He looked also under Barnes, thinking Terry might have used Mitch's name, but again found no birth date that matched or was even close to Hope's.

Hitting a dead end with the files, he turned to the computer on the records librarian's desk. A flashing icon demanded a password.

"Great," Dean muttered to himself. "If I had a few months or the right FBI software, I might be able to figure that out."

Prepared to give up, he glanced at a framed picture

of a gray-and-white cat displayed prominently on the desk. In scrolling letters formed from the stylized tail of a tiny mouse at the bottom of the frame was the name Snuggles.

He shook his head. "The woman couldn't be that stupid," he whispered, but on a hunch, typed the cat's name into the password block.

Amazed, he watched as the index for the hospital records appeared. It offered a choice of finding information by patient or doctor's name or by date. He typed in Kate's name and pulled up her patient list first. Then he entered the approximate date of Hope's birth. As the entries for late November materialized, Dean scanned them quickly, eliminating the ones with both parents listed. The name Mary Johnson appeared on the screen along with the notation of the time of birth of a baby girl, unnamed. No father. That was the extent of the computer information. Dean leapt from the chair and headed back toward the lateral files.

Mary Johnson's file was missing.

He swore under his breath. "I knew it wouldn't be that easy."

He returned to Bear, still waiting where he'd left her, and eased the door open a crack to survey the hall. It remained deserted.

"Looks like we'll have to check Kate's office, girl."

At the mention of Kate's name, Bear's tail wagging shifted into overdrive, shaking her entire hindquarters.

Dean sighed. "I know what you mean. I like her too—too damned much. Let's get this over with."

He started to open the door, but Bear gripped his wrist gently with her teeth. Just in time, he noticed someone rounding a corner at the far end of the hall. He closed the door and leaned against it, listening. The footsteps approached, then halted. Dean held his breath. Dylan would not be happy to bail one of his private investigators out of jail for breaking and entering. Dean could only hope the person in the hall wasn't headed for the records room.

A slight sound of splashing water traveled through the door, and Dean remembered seeing a water fountain midway down the hall. The splashing stopped, the footsteps resumed, then stopped again. The elevator dinged, and the doors slid open, then shut again. When Dean peered out, the hall was empty.

Moving quickly, he tugged Bear into the corridor with him and locked the records room door. Then he turned toward Kate's office, his last hope for finding a file marked Mary Johnson. The lock on her door was the same type as that of the records room, and he opened it easily. Bear followed him inside.

Drawing a deep breath of relief, Dean was stricken by a sudden inexplicable longing for Kate. Then he realized her subtle lilac fragrance lingered in the room. The scent set off the yearning he'd tried all day to squelch, and he shook his head in an attempt to clear his mind of images and memories of Kate. He couldn't work if he couldn't concentrate, and thoughts of the tantalizing Dr. Purvis blew his focus to bits.

He stationed Bear at the door once again. "Warn me if you hear anybody in the hall."

Next he surveyed the room. He'd headed for the filing cabinet in a corner, but a wall of photographs drew his attention and held it fast. Hundreds of pictures of smiling babies, some alone, others held by proud and beaming parents, were framed and mounted, filling the entire wall of one side of the room. Almost all were inscribed with high praise and affection for Dr. Purvis, or "Dr. Kate," as many of her patients called her. The sheer mass of baby humanity took his breath away. No wonder Kate loved her work. To bring so many lives into the world was like witnessing a perpetual miracle.

Remembering Hope, the baby whose father he was working for, Dean hurried to the file cabinet and pulled open a drawer. He found a Jennifer Johnson, and a Susan, but no Mary. Undeterred, he moved to Kate's desk in front of the wide window that overlooked the parking lot, and sat in her chair.

A laughing Kate with her arms around Mikey stared back at him from a framed eight-by-ten photo on her desktop. Guilt speared him as he realized how deeply he was betraying her trust, and only thoughts of Mitch Barnes and his daughter Hope, who needed her mother, kept Dean searching. He quickly glanced through the files neatly stacked on one corner of the desk, but found nothing. Tugging at the drawer on the right side, he found it locked.

With his picks, he leaned down, hidden behind the desk, and jimmied the mechanism. He was about to straighten when the office door opened and Kate's voice filled the room.

"Bear," she asked in surprise, "what are you doing here?"

Still hidden behind the desk, Dean suppressed a groan.

He'd been busted.

CHAPTER NINE

DEAN RIPPED OFF THE latex gloves and stuffed them behind Kate's desk. The traitorous Bear had moved to Kate's side, joyfully wagging her tail and licking Kate's hand as if the animal had never been so glad to see anyone in her short canine existence.

He grimaced at her betrayal. Some watchdog.

"What are you doing in my office?" Kate sputtered, surprise shifting to anger. "And how did you get in here?"

"I thought you were at the concert." Dean's mind was working fast, but for the life of him, he couldn't manufacture a story to get his head out of this noose.

"I intended to go, but the Albright baby decided to make an untimely arrival during the dinner hour." She swiveled, checking the room, bright medallions of anger coloring her cheeks. "What are you doing here?"

"It's a long story."

She pointed to Bear's harness. "And what's that?"

"Chapter Ten."

Her magnificent brown eyes widened as her suspicions blossomed. "You broke in, didn't you?"

"I didn't break anything. I simply unlocked the door."

As if her knees had suddenly given way, she collapsed in a chair in front of her desk. "You broke into my room at home, too, didn't you? *You* ruined my study."

"No—"

"No wonder you were so helpful about repairing the damage." Her voice leaped an octave. "Guilty conscience?"

"Kate, I swear—"

Heartbreak glistened in her eyes. "Why should I believe anything you say? You've lied to me about everything, haven't you?"

"Not everything. I—"

"I'm calling security." She shoved to her feet, hands shaking.

He pushed the phone across the desk toward her. "Go ahead. They'll come and take me away. Then you'll never hear my side of the story."

She tilted her chin in a defiant angle. "Why should I care?"

"Because what we shared last night *wasn't* a lie."

"It was only a kiss." Her lips trembled in denial of her words, and he hated himself for hurting her. "It didn't mean anything," she insisted, contradicting her earlier words at lunch.

He didn't believe her. "Can you look me in the eye and say that?"

Avoiding his gaze, she didn't answer.

"Please," he begged. "Give me a chance to explain. If you still want to call security after I'm finished, I won't stop you."

"And I'm supposed to take your word on that?" The irony in her voice cut deep, making him wince.

"Point taken. What if we go down to the waiting room? We can sit in a corner, I'll tell my story, and if you feel threatened or decide you still want to turn me in, all you have to do is raise your voice for help."

What he wanted more than anything was to kiss her again, to prove that what they'd shared the night before hadn't been a sham, but in her present state of mind, he doubted even the most sincere and passionate of kisses would melt the icy anguish in her eyes.

"What's to keep you from bolting and running once we reach the lobby?" she demanded.

He withdrew his keys from his jeans and tossed them to her. "I won't get far without my truck."

She caught the keys deftly and dropped them on her desk. "You're the type who keeps a spare set in a magnetic box under the fender."

With a sigh, he pulled out his wallet and handed it to her. "Will this help?"

"It's a start." She flipped the wallet open and scanned his driver's license. Her lips parted in surprise. "Your name really is Dean Harding."

"I told you, not everything's a lie. You'll find my private investigator's license in there, too. That's why I'm here. I'm working on a case."

Confusion clouded the silky bourbon-brown of her eyes. "What kind of case?"

"A missing person. Like I said, it's a long story."

She glanced at his P.I. license and the carry permit beneath it. "You have a gun?"

"In my boot. If it'll make you feel safer, I'll give you that, too."

She shook her head and sank into the chair again as if the burden of suspicion was too heavy to bear. Faint smears of violet shadows were visible beneath her eyes, and her body sagged with fatigue.

"Did you have dinner?" he asked gently, stricken with a tenderness he knew he had no right to feel.

She shook her head.

"Me, either. I noticed a diner next to the hospital. Weird name—Austin Eats. Let me buy you supper. I promise I'll tell you the whole story."

She lifted her head, ran her fingers through her thick hair to sweep it off her forehead, and gazed at him with doubt-filled eyes. "I don't trust you."

"I don't blame you. Look, we'll give my gun, wallet and keys to the security guard at the front door. You can tell him we're going to the diner, and if you're not back in an hour, he's to call the police."

"Are you crazy?" He could tell she was only half kidding.

He shrugged and forced a grin. "Have to be to hold this job."

"You said you're looking for a missing person. Who's your client?"

"A baby girl named Hope Barnes. You brought her into this world. Now I'm trying to find her mother."

Her eyes narrowed in distrust. "I don't remember delivering a child named Hope Barnes."

"Her mother used a false name. Probably gave the baby one, too."

He could almost see the wheels turning in her brain as she struggled with whether to believe him. Suddenly she set her jaw in a determined line and fixed him with a piercing stare. "I'll have dinner with you and listen to your story, but I'm still reserving the right to turn you in to the police for breaking and entering."

"Fair enough." His battle was half-won. Now all he had to do was convince her to tell him Terry Monteverde's whereabouts. And, equally important, to persuade her to forgive him for deceiving her. Knowing Kate as he did, he didn't know which task would be harder.

She shoved his wallet and keys back toward him. "Keep these. I know the owner of the diner, and everyone who works there. I'll feel safe enough."

Dean replaced his keys and wallet in his pocket, then hurried to follow Kate out of her office. He'd won one minor skirmish. He was a long way from winning the war.

FEELING AS IF she were moving through a bad dream, Kate accompanied Dean and Bear downstairs to the lobby. She couldn't believe the ironic and painful twist her life had taken. Just as she'd finally convinced herself to risk loving Dean, she'd stumbled onto his deception. At first, she'd resisted to save herself a broken heart. Now her worst fears had come to pass. She couldn't count on Dean Harding any more than she had been able to rely on her father or Steven.

She'd be double-dogged-damned, however, if she'd let him see how he'd hurt her.

Once outside the hospital, Dean removed Bear's harness, handed it to the dog and ordered the Lab to wait for him in the truck. Kate watched in amazed silence as Bear trotted across the parking lot with the harness between her teeth, bounded obediently into the truck bed, turned around several times and lay down with her head hanging over the tail gate, her sad eyes reproaching them for not taking her along.

Guilt tweaked Kate at the dog's dejected expression. *Of all the rotten luck. I've not only fallen hard for a handsome cowboy who's lied through his perfect white teeth, I've even gone loopy over his big, cuddly dog.*

Hurt and disgusted with herself, she turned without speaking and stomped next door to the diner.

The bright and cheerful Austin Eats was busiest during breakfast and lunch, but by this time of the evening, the place was almost empty. Joe, the elderly cook, waved to her from behind the counter, and Mary Jane, one of the regular waitresses, greeted her by name, showed them to a booth and handed them a menu.

"Today's special is meat loaf," Mary Jane announced.

"Just coffee." Kate had trouble forcing the words past the lump in her throat.

Since learning of Dean Harding's treachery, she wanted nothing more than to run home, lock herself in her room, hide under the covers and cry. She'd agreed to hear his story more to show him that his deception hadn't mattered than out of curiosity. She doubted anything he had to say could make up for the devastation she felt.

"Just coffee for me, too," Dean said.

He waited until Mary Jane had filled their cups and departed before speaking again. "I'm sorry. You have every right to be furious with me."

She sipped her coffee, but didn't reply. She still feared bursting into tears of anger as well as disappointment. The hot coffee scalded her throat and brought the unwanted tears to her eyes. She dashed them away with the back of her hand and fought to speak without a tremor in her voice. "Tell me about the baby."

Dean picked up his cup and shook his head. "That would be starting in the middle. The story begins with her father, Mitch Barnes. He's the man who hired Finders Keepers detective agency out of Trueblood, the people I work for. They specialize in locating missing persons."

She nodded, blew on her coffee, and took a more careful sip, wondering how far she could trust what Dean was saying. His employment should be easy enough to verify. Trueblood and the detective agency were only a phone call away.

"Mitch Barnes is a former FBI agent," Dean continued. "He was in Rio last year on a case during Carnival—"

"Rio, as in Brazil?"

Dean nodded. "He met a very beautiful and mysterious young woman and was drawn to her instantly. They shared a night of lovemaking, and Mitch felt he'd finally met the perfect woman for him. But she refused to tell her name. When morning came, she'd disappeared. All he had left to remember her by was a hazy Polaroid of her wearing her Carnival mask. He tried to find her before he left Brazil, but without any luck.''

In spite of her crushed feelings, Kate found her interest piqued by Dean's account. ''The baby was conceived that night?''

''Apparently. Last March, a four-month-old infant was left at the apartment building in San Antonio where Mitch was staying. Testing revealed that Mitch is definitely the baby's father.''

Kate's maternal instincts rebelled at the mother's desertion of her baby. ''The woman came all the way from Brazil to abandon her baby? I hope she had a damned good reason.''

''She did, but Mitch didn't know it at the time. Remember, he didn't know anything about her, not even her name. He was desperate to find her, so he contacted the Finders Keepers agency.''

''And they assigned you to the case.''

''Not at first. They contacted a guy in Brazil—Rick Singleton—and sent him a copy of the woman's picture. Through the jewelry the woman was wearing in the photo, he was able to trace her to the Monteverdes, a wealthy Brazilian family who run a business specializing in gems.''

"He found her? Then why are you still searching?"

Frowning, Dean pushed his fingers through his hair. "It's not that simple. Rick met the woman's sister, Nina, and discovered that a few months after Carnival, Terry Monteverde fled Brazil."

"Fled? Why?"

"She'd been accused of smuggling gems."

"She was a crook?"

The undeniable warmth of his slow grin bruised her already hurting heart with longing for what might have been. "Now you're getting ahead of me."

"Since you're still looking for her, I take it this Rick was unable to find her?"

Dean nodded. "And for good reason. Terry was reported killed in a boating accident."

Kate shook her head in an effort to clear her confusion. "You're searching for a *dead* woman?"

"She's very much alive. After Terry fled to this country, she faked her death."

"Why would she do that?"

"Leo Hayes, the real gem smuggler, believed Terry had taken off with a couple of his diamonds worth a large fortune. He was determined to find her, retrieve his gems, and kill her for inconveniencing him."

"Nice guy," Kate said with an ironic grimace, and sipped her coffee, fascinated in spite of herself by Terry Monteverde's story.

"Not nice at all," Dean said. "In reality, about as mean and nasty as they come. Terry fabricated her own drowning in a boating accident to protect herself from Hayes. A friend here in Texas helped her pull off the sham. Her friend wasn't even aware Terry was pregnant."

"But what about her baby?"

"We're assuming Terry left the baby with Mitch to protect her, in case Hayes managed to track Terry down. Mitch is the child's father. What better protection could a kid want?"

Kate's head hurt as she tried to follow the twists and turns of Dean's bizarre story. His tale had to be true. Who could make up such an escapade?

"So you're attempting to find Terry Monteverde before Leo Hayes does?"

He shook his head. "Leo Hayes is dead."

Dean's story became more fantastic with each new fact. "Really dead?" she asked with a touch of sarcasm. "Or is he faking his death, too?"

"He's dead all right. Killed by a Texas Ranger when Hayes threatened the life of the friend who'd helped Terry fake her drowning."

"So with Leo Hayes dead, Terry's hiding now to avoid the law because of the charges against her?"

"Terry probably doesn't know Leo's dead. And from what Rick learned in Rio, Terry's innocent, though of course she'll have to prove that to the Brazilian authorities. Looks like someone tried to frame her with the embezzlement and smuggling charges."

Kate leaned back in the booth, crossed her arms over her chest, and fixed him with a withering stare. "Okay, so I know *why* you're trying to find this Terry

Monteverde. But you still haven't explained what you were doing in my office."

Once more, his slow, easy smile was like a knife in her heart. "You're getting ahead of me again."

Steeling herself to remain in his all too arresting company for a while longer, she nodded. "So what happened next?"

"That's when Finders Keepers hired me to locate Terry."

Kate shook her head in disbelief. "Even if Terry's still in Texas, it's a big place. Isn't searching for her like looking for a needle in a haystack?"

"It would be, except we have a starting place."

She raised an eyebrow. "Austin?"

"Bingo."

She folded her arms on the table and leaned toward him. "I don't get it. What makes you think this baby was born here and that I delivered her?"

"We had a few solid facts to help us search. The baby's approximate birth date—"

"Extrapolated from the date of her conception?"

"Right. We also know her ethnicity and blood type."

"Not much to go on," Kate said. "Do you realize how many babies are born in Texas every day? Has to be close to a thousand."

"We lucked out," Dean said. "I discovered a professor at the University of Texas doing research on factors that influence the birth weight of infants. He had already accumulated the statistics of every baby born in eastern Texas during the time period when

Hope would have arrived, along with their ethnicity, blood type, place of birth and attending obstetrician.''

Frustrated and angry, Kate sighed. "If you have all you need, why come to me?"

"The stats didn't include the babies' names," Dean explained. "Through the process of elimination, I've identified every other baby born around Hope's birth date. There's little doubt, Kate, that you delivered her and that the baby is Terry Monteverde's child."

Kate leaned back against the seat. "I don't get it. If you have what you need, why come here?" Her eyes narrowed with hurt and accusation. "Why the aw-shucks cowboy routine and renting the room at our house under false pretenses?"

"I tried calling the hospital. Talked with the records librarian and your secretary. Both refused to give out any information."

"They would have lost their jobs if they had."

"All I needed was Terry's address. If you could see that adorable little girl and how much her daddy loves her, you'd bend a few rules, too, to reunite them with her mother."

Dean's gray eyes had softened with wistfulness when he mentioned the child, and Kate realized with a start that this wasn't just a job for him. He was committed to reuniting that family. She wondered if his resolve to put mother and child together grew out of memories of his own lonely childhood with his Aunt Carrie. Her attitude toward him was softening—until she remembered the destruction at the boarding-house. Maybe the poignant stories of his unhappy boyhood had been lies, too, meant to make her more susceptible to his charms.

"So you trashed my study at home, looking for Terry's address?"

"No!" He grabbed her hand before she could pull it away and skewered her with a look she couldn't avoid. "I'm through lying to you, Kate. Since the first day I saw you, I've regretted my deception, but, with God as my witness, I did not vandalize your study."

"Of course not," she said with a bite in her tone. "You're just a humble private investigator with all the skills of a cat burglar and a con artist."

He squeezed her hand gently. "Remember how I found you on the porch the night of the break-in?"

She nodded. Every moment she'd spent with him had been burned indelibly into her mind.

"I'd just come from searching your study. I admit I picked the lock to get in, but I damaged nothing and left the room exactly as I found it."

"Then who—?"

"I have some theories," he said, "but let me finish this story first."

Startled to discover her hand still nestled in his, she jerked it away. "I'm listening."

God help her, she wanted to do more than listen. She wanted to throw herself into his arms, feel his body against hers, experience again the bone-shaking passion of the kiss they'd shared last night. She had to be crazy. She wanted him in spite of the fact that he'd lied and that the sole reason for his presence in her life was to help him solve his case.

"Are you?" he asked.

She pulled herself from her traitorous thoughts. "What?"

"Listening? You looked as if you were a thousand miles away."

Not miles away, she thought ruefully. She was too blasted close for her own good. She had to let him finish his story so she could escape. How could she forget his charm while he sat within reach, reminding her of all the things she needed to forget? "I assume since you didn't find Terry's address in my study, you decided to try my office at the hospital."

"I looked in the records room first. I was able to access the computer files and discovered that Terry might have used the name Mary Johnson."

The name clicked immediately in her memory, bringing to mind a beautiful woman with thick, dark hair and sad, almond-shaped eyes.

"You remember her, don't you?" Dean asked.

"Not offhand." She didn't like lying, but he deserved it, especially after all he'd put her through. "I deliver a lot of babies."

"I know. I saw the pictures on your wall. That's some rogues' gallery you've got there. You must be very proud of the work you do."

Admiration shone in his gray eyes, and she tore her gaze away, focusing on the cook, reading the newspaper behind the counter.

"All I need," Dean said, "is an address. I have to let Terry know that Leo Hayes is dead and it's safe for her to see her baby again."

Conflicting emotions warred within her. Even if releasing information about a patient wasn't an ethical issue, she hated giving Dean what he asked, especially since he'd gone about getting it in such an underhanded way. On the other hand, she wanted to reunite the mother with her baby. She remembered Mikey as an infant and how devastated she'd have felt if she'd been separated from him for all those precious months.

"I know you're angry with me," Dean said, "but I'm not asking for myself. I'm asking for Hope and Terry and Mitch. They deserve to be a family."

She wanted to believe him, but she couldn't help being skeptical. "If she left him the baby, she knows where he lives. She could contact him if she wanted to be found."

"But she still believes there's a killer on her trail."

With his easy smile and tempting eyes, he was so persuasive, she was almost convinced. But while her heart prompted her to trust him, her intellect waved caution flags. For all she knew, seducing her had been part of his plan to obtain information. She needed time and distance to sort out her feelings—and to check out the amazing Mr. Harding. "I don't give out a patient's information without her permission."

"Okay, don't give me her address. But there's nothing to stop you from contacting her and telling her Leo Hayes is dead and she can come out of hiding."

Kate shook her head. "There is something to stop me."

He cocked his head. "More ethical problems?"

"No."

"Then what?"

"I have her Austin address, but I can't reach her there."

"Why not?"

Certainly she could do no harm telling him where the woman *wasn't*. "Mary, or Terry, as you call her, left Austin not long after her baby was born."

He didn't bother to hide his disappointment. "Are you sure?"

"She stopped by the house with the baby to thank me and to say goodbye. Said she was leaving Austin for good."

"Did she say where she was going?"

Kate shook her head.

"Please," he begged. "At least give me her last known residence. Maybe she left a forwarding address there."

"I don't—" The vibration of the beeper on her belt interrupted her, and she glanced at the digital display. "The hospital's calling me. I have to leave."

"I'll go with you."

"Not necessary." She slid out of the booth and headed for the door.

He caught her hand as she tried to pass. "I haven't finished the rest of the story. Don't you want to hear my theories on who trashed your study?"

She pulled free and kept walking.

Dean peeled several dollars out of his pocket, flung them on the table, and followed her.

"If another baby's on the way," she called over her shoulder as she left the diner, "you could be in for a long wait."

The humid summer air hit her in the face like a damp blanket and made breathing difficult, but she forced herself to hurry through the muggy atmosphere. In the distance, she could hear sirens, possibly an ambulance. If a mother and baby were in distress and on their way to Maitland, she wanted to be waiting when they arrived.

With two long strides, Dean caught up with her. "I'm a patient man."

She glanced at him sideways, irritated by the amicable grin on his handsome face. If he felt guilty for deceiving her, it didn't show. Ignoring him, she sprinted up the sweeping front walk and entered the main door.

A security guard rushed to meet her. "Glad you're here, Dr. Purvis. The police are on their way."

His words stopped her cold. "Police? What's happened?" Her first thoughts were of Mikey and her mother. "My family—"

"Nothing to do with your family," he reassured her.

"What's the problem then?" Dean took her arm, and forgetting her anger for the moment, she welcomed his support.

The security guard jerked a thumb toward the second floor. "It's your office, ma'am. Somebody's turned the place upside down."

She turned to glare at Dean. He'd wounded her

confidence in him so deeply, she couldn't help wondering if he'd lured her away while an accomplice completed what he started.

"Don't look at me like that," he said. "I have a watertight alibi. I was with you, remember?"

"Maybe you don't work alone."

Instead of being angered by her accusation, he surprised her by laughing. "Bear's good, but she's not that good." His expression sobered. "My bet is that whoever broke into your home study followed through here."

Her head and heart ached from emotional whiplash as she vacillated between trusting him and not. "Why is this happening?"

Taking her elbow, he led her gently toward the elevator. "We'll know more once the police check your office, but my gut says someone besides me is looking for Terry Monteverde."

CHAPTER TEN

THE DOUBT in her eyes hurt, but Dean had expected as much. Kate Purvis was a smart cookie, not one to be led blindly by any man, no matter how strongly she was attracted to him. He had his work cut out for him, getting her to believe in him again. She'd have to trust him to give him Terry Monteverde's Austin address, but finding Terry had taken second place to his desire for Kate's approval.

His hand still on Kate's elbow, he stopped her at the sound of tires screeching to a halt outside the lobby entrance. They turned to see two uniformed officers enter and speak with the security guard.

"We should wait and let them check things out first," Dean said. "They won't want us in your office before the crime scene unit does their job."

She gazed up at him with worried eyes. "I need to see how bad it is."

"Okay." He gave her arm a reassuring squeeze. The officers were approaching the elevator, and Dean called to them. "This is Dr. Purvis. It's her office that was broken into. Can we come along and take a look?"

The officers exchanged glances. "As long as you

don't touch anything,'' the shorter one said. ''Maybe the doc can tell us if anything's missing.''

Dean and Kate stepped into the elevator with the officers, got off at the second floor, and followed the policemen down the hall. Kate's office door stood ajar, and the short officer took a moment to inspect it.

''Definitely not a professional,'' he commented. ''Whoever did this really butchered the lock.''

His partner stepped inside, then joined Dean and Kate in the hall. ''You can go in, ma'am. Just don't touch anything.''

Kate glanced at Dean, her face pale, her eyes a kaleidoscope of emotions from fear to anger and accusation. Straightening her shoulders as if prepared for the worst, she stepped into the center of her office and surveyed the damage. Dean watched from the doorway.

The drawers of the filing cabinet in the corner stood open and files were flung across the room, folders standing open on the floor like the wings of injured birds. Her desktop had been swiped clean, its contents scattered on the carpet.

Kate circled the desk and gazed down. ''Looks like someone tried to jimmy the lock on my desk drawer, but they must have been interrupted. It's still intact.''

''The other drawers?'' Dean asked.

''They're emptied, but looks like the contents were dumped, not taken.''

Her voice was breathless with shock, and Dean longed to comfort her. Her suspicions of him were too sharp and fresh for her to appreciate his concern, though, so he waited in the hall with his arms crossed over his chest and his hands tucked beneath his armpits.

"Can you tell if anything's been taken?" the short cop asked.

Stepping back into the corridor, Kate shook her head. "I'll have to reconstruct my file folders before I can answer that."

"Looks like whoever it was must have been after somebody's records," the other cop commented.

Kate looked at Dean, and he nodded with an I-told-you-so expression.

At the ding of the elevator, the doors slid open, and a familiar-looking, tall, lanky man with dark-rimmed glasses, a rumpled summer suit, and the ascetic features of a monk or a classics professor stepped off. The officers hurried to meet him, and the trio spoke quietly for a few minutes. When they'd finished, the uniformed officers entered the elevator and descended to the first floor.

The thin man approached Dean and Kate. "I'm Detective Marston. The crime scene unit is on its way."

"Kate Purvis. This is my office."

"I'm Dean Harding."

The detective studied Dean for a moment. "San Antonio PD. Homicide, right?"

Suddenly remembering where he'd met the man before, Dean nodded. "We worked together on that interstate serial killer case several years ago."

Kate's jaw dropped for an instant before she caught

herself and clamped it shut, eyes narrowed on Dean. "You were a policeman?"

The warmth of Marston's smile smoothed the craggy angles of his face. "More than just a policeman, Dr. Purvis. Harding here was the best damned detective on the San Antonio force." He turned to Dean. "You left the job?"

"Several years ago. Bought a little ranch in the hill country."

Marston scowled. "Gave up investigating?"

Dean shook his head. "Not altogether. I freelance sometimes for the Finders Keepers agency out of Trueblood."

Marston nodded. "Dylan and Lily Garrett. They have excellent reputations."

"This looks like a simple B and E," Dean said. "Why are the Austin police sending out their top gun?"

"The Maitlands do a lot of good work in this community," Marston said. "Any problem at the hospital and we're all over it like a cheap suit." He turned to Kate and jerked his head toward her office. "Any idea who might have done this?"

Dean wouldn't have been surprised if Kate had named him as the chief suspect, but she merely shook her head. She looked exhausted, she hadn't eaten, and between her usual killer schedule, Mikey's recent escapade, and the break-in at her house, she'd been through hell the past few days.

Dean's protective instincts kicked in. He indicated a grouping of chairs in a waiting area at the end of the hall. "Let's sit down. Kate's had a rough few days, Marston, and this hasn't helped."

She bristled at his concern. "Don't patronize me."

"You're the doctor." Dean shrugged and waved her toward a chair. "At least take a load off your feet."

She looked as if she wanted to protest again, but the fight seemed to leave her like the air from a punctured balloon. She sagged onto a sofa, appearing fragile and exhausted despite the inner strength Dean had noted from the first time they met. Marston took the chair closest to her, and Dean sat on her other side.

"From the way the file cabinet was torn apart," Dean told the detective, "I'd guess someone's looking for info on one of Kate's patients."

Marston looked to Kate, who nodded in agreement. "I won't know if any files are missing," she said, "until I've had a chance to go through them."

"Are you aware of any patients who've had problems recently?" Marston asked.

Kate frowned. "Medical problems?"

The detective shook his head. "Personal problems. A messy divorce, paternity suit, that kind of thing."

Dean watched the detective put Kate at ease with his calm tone and relaxed manner. From the rough planes of his face to the imperfect cut of his clothes to the sympathetic warmth of nearsighted blue eyes behind Coke-bottle lenses, he looked more like a model for a Norman Rockwell painting than an astute detective with a reputation for closing cases that reached the length and breadth of Texas.

Kate glanced at Dean, then turned back to Marston. "There is one patient who's in trouble."

Marston leaned back in his chair. "Maybe you'd better fill me in from the beginning."

As quickly as possible, Dean related the story of Mitch Barnes and Terry Monteverde, including the death of Leo Hayes.

"Let me get this straight," Marston said. "You're trying to locate this Monteverde woman to reunite her with her husband and baby."

"Right," Dean said.

"And the man who was after her is dead?"

"Killed by a Texas Ranger when he threatened another woman's life."

Marston frowned. "If this Hayes fellow is dead, what makes you think someone else is looking for Terry Monteverde besides you?"

"Seems too much of a coincidence," Dean said, "that I come to Austin searching for Terry, and both places I search are subsequently broken into by someone else. It's almost as if someone is following my lead."

"Any idea who?" Marston asked.

"I had suspected Raoul Davega—"

"Raoul?" Kate sputtered in surprise. "Why Raoul?"

Marston raised his eyebrows again.

"Raoul," Dean explained, "was a boarder at Kate's mother's home. He disappeared the morning after Kate's study was vandalized. Dylan Garrett contacted the airlines and discovered Raoul had flown to

Rio de Janeiro, Terry Monteverde's hometown. I suspected at the time Raoul might be an associate of Hayes's that we weren't aware of."

"But you don't suspect him now?" Marston asked.

"Unless he turned around and caught a flight back to the States," Dean explained, "he couldn't have broken in here at the hospital."

Kate moaned and covered her face with her hands. "All these suspicions are making me dizzy."

Again, Dean resisted the desire to put his arm around her and draw her close. "Dylan has an associate in Rio trailing Raoul. We can check quickly enough whether the guy is still out of the country."

Marston removed his glasses and cleaned them with his tie, then held them up to the light for inspection. "There's always the possibility these break-ins aren't related to the Monteverde woman at all." He replaced his glasses slightly askew.

"But if they are," Dean said, "I need to find her before someone else does."

Kate lifted her head, her bourbon-colored eyes wide with alarm. "You think someone wants to harm her?"

"I doubt they're from some sweepstakes contest with a prize check," Dean said with a twisted grin. "Maybe they're after the jewels Terry allegedly took from Hayes."

Footsteps sounded down the corridor, and Dean glanced up to see a woman approach. Attractive with dark hair, she wore delivery-room scrubs, identifying her as another doctor. She rushed toward Kate as soon as she spotted her.

"What's going on?" the newcomer asked. "Security alerted me there's been a break-in."

"My office." Kate introduced Abby Maitland McDermott, the hospital's chief of staff, to Marston and Dean.

When Kate identified Dean by name, Abby offered an innuendo-laden, "Oh."

That one word indicated Kate had mentioned Dean to her boss before, but in what context, Dean wasn't able to tell. He couldn't miss the critical scrutiny the chief of staff gave him when she thought he wasn't looking, though.

After striding to the door of Kate's office for an assessment of the situation, Abby returned to the group in the waiting area.

"I'll send in a couple of clerks tomorrow to reassemble and file your patient folders," Abby announced.

"I can do it myself," Kate protested.

Her boss shook her head. "Tomorrow's Saturday, and you're not on call this weekend. By the time you get back Monday, we should have a handle on what files, if any, are missing, once we've compared what's in your office with your computerized patient list."

Marston beamed approval. "Very efficient, Doctor. If files are missing, I'll want to be informed."

"Of course," Abby agreed.

Dean wanted to know, too, but he held his tongue. His money was betting that the Mary Johnson file was still locked in the bottom right-hand drawer of Kate's desk and only an act of Congress or an act of God would move her to share its contents with him.

"So," KATE ASKED the next day, "which are you, a cop or a cowboy?"

Dean kept his eyes on the road ahead, watching for the turnoff to the Double G Ranch. "Does it make a difference?"

Kate shrugged. "None. Just fishing for a straight answer for a change."

The Saturday afternoon sun glinted off the hood of his pickup, and Dean appreciated his sunglasses, not only to protect him from the glare but to hide the gleam in his eyes from the passenger pressed intimately against his side.

Sitting next to him hadn't been her idea. If she'd had her choice, she'd have been hugging the passenger door, he was certain. Mikey, however, in his exuberance over his first visit to an honest-to-goodness Texas ranch, had insisted on riding shotgun with Bear, who was having the time of her life with her head hanging out the window and the breeze blowing her fur like a fashion model's hair in a wind tunnel. Doggy heaven.

At every curve in the road, in spite of her seat belt and her obvious efforts to stay put, Kate slid against him, the warm softness of her thigh burning through his jeans and the sweet curve of her breast brushing his arm and revving his already overactive fantasies into an overdrive that threatened to blow his engines.

In his efforts to extract Terry Monteverde's Austin address from Kate, Dean had decided to pull out the big guns. He'd asked Dylan to invite Mitch and Hope to the Double G for the afternoon. He was taking Kate and Mikey to meet them all at the ranch. If the sight of the adorable motherless little girl and Mitch's obvious desire to locate Terry didn't crack Kate's strict adherence to medical ethics, Dean didn't know what would.

Besides, he was happy for the excuse to spend the day with Kate and Mikey. Tooling down the highway, they looked like any other family on a weekend outing, and he savored the image.

Not that he had a snowball's chance in hell of Kate ever going out with him on a real date again. He'd noted the distrust in her eyes and the pinched expression of her mouth when she looked at him, and he couldn't fault her for her doubts. He'd misrepresented himself to her and her family, had lied a dozen times over, and she'd caught him red-handed rifling through her office. She'd already been hurt by her father and Mikey's dad. Instead of rebuilding her faith in men, Dean had added the final straw.

He doubted she'd have agreed to today's trip if Mikey hadn't overheard the offer and lit up like a Christmas tree. She'd have needed a stone heart to turn the kid down, and if there was one thing Kate Purvis wasn't, it was hard-hearted, especially where her son was concerned.

"Well?" Kate's question broke his reverie.

"Deep subject." Dean covered being caught day-dreaming with a lame joke and a grin.

"Yeah," Mikey piped in, "are you going to tell us?"

"Tell you what, sport?"

"What you are," Mikey insisted. "A cowboy or a cop?"

"Can't I be both?" Dean asked.

"A cowboy cop?" Mikey asked in awe.

"Sure," Dean said. "Most people aren't just one thing or another. Take your mother, for example. She's a mom and a doctor. And there's your nana. She runs a boardinghouse and is a cook and a grandma, too."

"What about me?" Mikey asked. "I'm just a kid."

"You're much more than that." Dean felt Kate's gaze fastened on him and chose his words carefully. "You're a son and a grandson and a friend to your pals. So you see, it's hard to classify someone by just one thing."

"How would you classify yourself?" Kate asked Dean.

"Several years ago, I'd have said I was a husband and a cop, but things change. Now I'm primarily a rancher who works a little as an investigator on the side."

"Do you like investigating?" she asked.

"Some of it. Other parts aren't so hot."

"Like what?"

"Like having to mislead people to find out what I need to know. Dishonesty's against my nature—"

"But you do it so well." Her voice dripped with irony.

"Investigating?" he asked, deliberately misunderstanding her.

"Misleading. You'd make a great actor."

He grinned. "Suppose Naomi could find me a part at the dinner theater?"

"Do you sing?" Mikey asked. "I've seen singing cowboys on television."

"Singing's not one of my strong points," Dean admitted.

"What is your strong point?" Kate asked, as if doubtful he had one.

"Stick-to-itiveness." He lowered his sunglasses and gazed at her over the top of them. "When I go after something, I don't give up until I get it."

"If you're talking about Mary Johnson's address—"

"Not necessarily. I'm talking about a lot of things."

He turned his attention back to the highway, but not before having the satisfaction of observing her blush at the implications in his words. He may have struck out until now with Kate, but as far as he was concerned, the game wasn't over yet.

"Are you a daddy?" Mikey asked out of the blue.

"No," Dean said.

"Would you like to be?" the boy persisted.

Kate stiffened at the boy's question. "Mikey, I don't think—"

"It's okay," Dean said. "Yes, Mikey, I'd like to be a daddy some day."

"Would you be my daddy?"

"Mikey!" Kate blurted.

"But, Mom, I don't have one, and all my friends do."

A quick glance at Kate revealed her color had deepened to beet-red.

"Sorry, Mikey," Dean said, "but it's up to your mother to choose a dad for you."

"Why?"

Dean laughed. "Because mothers are in charge of everything. Haven't you learned that by now?"

"We'll talk about this later, Mikey," Kate said quickly, as if to ward off further embarrassment from her son's comments.

Dean couldn't help thinking how closely the boy's thoughts paralleled his own of the three of them and Bear as a real family. Earlier he'd been anxious to return to the solitude of his ranch. Now he dreaded the prospect of its loneliness and isolation.

"Are we almost there?" Mikey asked for the umpteenth time since they'd left Austin.

Dean slowed the truck and swung onto the road that led to the Double G. "Almost. The Garretts keep horses in this front pasture. Why don't you see how many you can count?"

ON THE BROAD front veranda of the Double G, William waited with Mitch for Dean's arrival with the Austin doctor. They'd left Hope in the office, peacefully asleep in a portable crib, while Lily and Dylan went over the month's financial reports for the agency.

At a glance, Mitch appeared relaxed, pushing the weather-worn rocker back and forth with the toe of his boot, but his tension was evident in the white-knuckled grip of his fingers on the chair arms and the tick of a muscle in his jaw.

"It'll be okay," William assured him. "One look at Hope, and Dr. Purvis won't be able to resist helping us find her mother."

"I hope you're right." Mitch released his death grip on the chair and pushed his fingers through his hair in obvious frustration.

William tried a change of subject. "Congratulations. Dylan told me the job with the sheriff's department is yours if you want it. When would you start?"

"Not till the fall. I need time to find a nanny for Hope."

"A nanny?" William frowned at the idea. "Wouldn't she be happier staying here with us? Between Lily and me, we could take good care of her."

Mitch shook his head. "Lily has her own baby, and besides, I've imposed on you folks enough already. I couldn't—"

William shook his head. "Having Hope is always a pleasure, not an imposition." In a sudden attack of nerves, he cleared his throat and prepared to broach the subject he'd been gathering courage for all afternoon, but in the end, that courage failed him. As he and Mitch sat together in a companionable silence, William let his memories drift back to almost forty years ago. His father had died, and, overwhelmed by his loss and scared spitless at the responsibility of running the ranch, William had fled.

In his mind's eye he saw the troubled young man he'd been, drifting through Oklahoma and Texas, taking one job after another, never staying in any one place for long, until he ended up in Laredo, where he'd met Bobby Jo Scott, Mitch's mother.

William couldn't help smiling. He'd had some good times with Bobby Jo, six months of them, to be exact, until one morning he woke up and realized he couldn't run from his responsibilities any longer. It was time to go home. Within a few weeks of returning to the ranch, he'd met Elizabeth Reilly, the love of his life, and within two months, they were married.

But how could he tell the proud young man beside him that he was his father? A father who'd abandoned him before he was born.

William sighed. He'd had no idea Bobby Jo was pregnant when he'd left her. To say he'd been shocked when he'd heard Mitch talking to Dean about his mother would be an understatement. But once William knew, he had started his own investigation. Mitch had signed a medical release when he agreed to have Dean look for his father, allowing access to the records they'd used to prove that Hope was Mitch's daughter. William had gone into San Antonio, had a few tests run on himself, then had them compared with Mitch's. The results had come back yesterday—DNA, blood type, the whole works.

Mitch was his son.

William stared at the handsome young man with a mix of emotions. When Dylan, Lily, and his youngest daughter, Ashley, had been growing up, William had been there for them. From scraped knees to chicken pox, from school plays to sporting events, from graduations to marriage, his children had been able to count on his love and support. Mitch, however, had grown up without the love and support of a father. Hell, the poor kid hadn't even known who his father *was,* and the knowledge filled William with sadness and shame.

Balancing those emotions was a fierce pride in Mitch's achievements. Bobby Jo had done a hell of a job as a single mother. Mitch had grown into a fine man, with rock-solid values, a strong sense of himself, and the admiration and respect of his peers in law enforcement.

But somehow the time wasn't right to tell Mitch. There were so many uncertainties in his life as it was, and all his energy and emotion needed to be spent in the search for Hope's mother.

William felt his eyes brim with tears. A new son. A new grandchild. He only hoped when he did tell Mitch that his son would feel even a fraction of the joy that filled William's heart at the knowledge of his newfound family.

The sound of a vehicle approaching brought Mitch to his feet and jarred William from his thoughts. He glanced behind him to see Dean's pickup nearing the house. He slung his arm over Mitch's shoulder. "The most important thing now is to find Hope's mother. Let's go meet Dr. Purvis."

CHAPTER ELEVEN

IN THE GREAT ROOM of the Double G, Dean had the luxury of studying Kate while Mitch related his story of meeting Terry Monteverde, losing her and then finding Hope in his apartment building. Emotions shifted and flitted across her perfect face at each turn of the story, and tears occasionally glittered in her magnificent eyes.

At first Dean felt like a jerk, allowing Mitch to manipulate Kate's sentiments so blatantly, but the more Dean thought about Terry Monteverde's plight and what he'd learned about Kate, the more certain he was that Kate would want the whole story. She wasn't the kind of woman who made decisions without knowing all the facts.

Dean hoped that trait would eventually aid in pleading his own case with Kate, if she'd let herself get to know him better.

William had already led an enthusiastic Mikey to the barn to view the foals, and Kate sat now in one of the oversize chairs cuddling Hope, sound asleep, on her shoulder.

"Is she too heavy?" Mitch interrupted his narrative to ask. "I can take her."

Kate shook her head and replied softly, "She's fine. I like holding her."

Dean was glad Mitch hadn't retrieved his daughter. He loved watching Kate with the baby in her arms. She looked like a Renaissance painter's madonna, radiating light and contentment with a beauty that was breathtaking. She was the kind of woman who was meant to have children. She'd already proved her extraordinary mothering skills, raising Mikey as a single parent, and Dean couldn't help but wonder if she ever longed for more children.

His children.

The ache in his groin was more than physical. It reached to his heart and an emptiness there that needed filling. Those thoughts, coming out of left field, startled him, stabbed him with unexpected longing. But the more he considered having children with Kate, the more right the idea seemed. He'd already pictured Kate and Mikey and him as a family. The prospect of having a baby with her totally preoccupied him—until reality kicked in and reminded him that Kate had good reason not to trust him, a serious impediment to any possibility of a lasting relationship.

Accepting defeat would have been the path of least resistance, but now that he'd found Kate Purvis, had tasted her kisses, had witnessed her competence and fierce devotion as both a mother and a doctor, he wasn't about to let her go. If it took a year of Sundays, he would find a way to make her trust him again....

His daydream bubble burst. For the life of him, he couldn't think how to regain her faith in him.

Mitch was also watching Kate closely. "My daughter needs her mother. Won't you help us, Dr. Purvis?"

Her eyes mirroring her inner struggle, Kate smoothed Hope's dark curls with slender fingers. "Even if I give you Terry's last known address, you have no guarantee you'll find her."

Mitch leaned forward, hands clasped between his knees. "But at least we'll have a starting place. Dean's one of the best investigators around, and he knows East Texas like the back of his hand. If he can't find Terry, no one can."

Kate cast Dean a sidelong glance. "I'll admit his methods are...unorthodox."

Dean grimaced. "That's a nice way of putting it, I suppose. Look, Kate, I'm sorry I broke into your office—"

"You should be. You're supposed to uphold the law, not break it." Her eyes flashed with disapproval.

"Sometimes," Dean replied, "you have to put people above the letter of the law, and you're holding my motivation in your arms. Would *you* let a few locks stop you from trying to find this baby's mom?"

Kate smiled, and the sweetness of it wrenched Dean's gut. Her loving expression was for the baby, but he'd have traded forty acres of his Texas hill country to be the recipient of such a look.

Her expression sobered when she lifted her eyes to meet Mitch's intense gaze. "What if Terry Monte-

verde doesn't want to be found? What if she knows
about Leo Hayes's death and she's avoiding you on
purpose?"

Mitch looked shocked. "You think she doesn't
want her own child?"

Kate shook her head. "She bonded instantly with
Hope when she was born. I witnessed that. And I saw
Terry with the baby before she left Austin when she
stopped to say goodbye. She adores this child. Being
away from Hope is probably breaking her heart."

"Then she'll be grateful if you help us find her,"
Dean suggested gently, "and reunite her with her
daughter."

Kate appeared torn, and Dean understood the dilemma she faced. Did she follow her feelings as a
mother or her ethics as a doctor?

"Ethics and laws are there for a reason," she insisted. "If you start bending them, eventually they
break."

"Aw jeez, Kate." Dean's patience was wearing
thin. "We're not talking about committing murder or
overthrowing the government. All we want is a simple address."

Her jaw set with a stubbornness that would have
been appealing if it hadn't been so damned frustrating. "It's the domino theory. 'For want of a shoe, the
horse was lost, for want of a horse—'"

"It's just a damned address—" Dean dragged his
fingers through his hair, resisting the urge to tear out
a few clumps "—not a state secret."

Mitch came to Kate's rescue. "If you help us find

Terry, Dr. Purvis, I promise I won't harass her. I'll leave her alone if she doesn't want me. But Hope deserves to know her mother. Believe me, I have first-hand experience of growing up not knowing one of my parents. It leaves a hole in your heart no one and nothing else can fill." No one could doubt the sincerity of the ex-FBI agent's words. That pain was etched too clearly on his face.

"There's another factor to consider." Dylan Garrett had joined them in the great room, and Dean introduced him to Kate.

"What other factor is there, Mr. Garrett?" Kate asked.

"Call me Dylan," he said with a grin. "I always think of my father as Mr. Garrett." His expression turned serious. "From what Dean's told us, it appears someone else is also searching for Terry Monteverde. We had assumed that Leo Hayes operated alone, but now I'm not so sure."

"Any word on Raoul Davega?" Dean asked.

Dylan shook his head. "Our operative in Rio lost him. He's tried the airlines, but if Raoul left the country, it was under an assumed name."

A frown creased the flawlessness of Kate's face. "So Terry Monteverde may still be in danger?"

"I'm afraid so," Dylan said.

Mitch focused his intense gaze on Kate. "If we find her first, we can protect her until whoever's after her is caught."

Dean turned to Kate, his voice soft. "Isn't your main objective as a doctor to save lives?"

Kate flashed him a crooked smile that twisted his heart. "Our oath states that, first and foremost, we do no harm."

Dean threw his hands in the air. "What harm could helping us do?"

"What if my giving you Terry's Austin address somehow leads her stalker to her?"

"And what if you *don't* tell us," Dean insisted, "and he finds her before we do? If he's working for Hayes, he'll kill her. A dead woman makes a lousy mother."

At that moment, Hope awoke in Kate's arms, leaned back, and with dark eyes shining, smiled at Kate, and patted the doctor's cheek with a chubby hand.

"She needs her mother," Mitch pleaded. "And she needs her mother alive and well."

Fearing another outright refusal, Dean jumped in before Kate could say anything. "You don't have to make up your mind now, but while I have you and Mitch together, there's something the two of you can do to help my investigation."

"But—" Kate began.

"It has nothing to do with doctor-patient privilege," Dean hastened to add, crossing his fingers and hoping that he was right. "Since we're so close to San Antonio, I'd like you both to visit the police department. Between the two of you, you can supply a good description of Terry to the forensics artist. If we can come up with an accurate picture, finding her will be a whole lot easier."

Mitch turned to Kate with a worried expression. "You have a problem with that? You've seen her more recently than I have, so your impressions will be fresher."

"I don't know...." Kate wrinkled her forehead. "I'm not wild about dragging Mikey into a police station."

"Leave him with Dad and me," Dylan suggested. "We'll keep a good eye on him—my sister Lily can help—and he'll enjoy seeing more of the ranch."

"I can vouch for the Garretts as baby-sitters," Mitch assured her. "Hope stays here often."

Kate turned to Dean with a what-have-you-gotten-me-into look. "I suppose it will be okay, as long as we're not gone too long."

"Good," Dean said before she could change her mind. "Let's find Mikey and tell him where we're going."

A FEW MILES NORTH of San Antonio, Kate was still mentally kicking herself for agreeing to the excursion. Not that she minded helping create a sketch of Terry Monteverde. If someone found Terry ahead of Dean and harmed her, Kate didn't want that responsibility on her shoulders.

What bothered her most about the trip into the city was the proximity to Dean Harding. With gentlemanly gallantry, Mitch had insisted on opening the passenger door of Dean's pickup and helping Kate inside. She'd ended up sandwiched between the two handsome lawmen, squeezed as close to Dean as she'd been during the entire trip to the Double G. Enduring that close contact brought back memories of every time he'd touched her and the way he'd kissed her, until her bones felt like molten wax and her pulse, respiration rate, body temperature and sanity threatened to blow through the roof of the cab. How could her emotions be stirred so wildly by a man who'd proved he couldn't be trusted?

In an attempt to ignore her tingling response to Dean, she turned toward Mitch. "Did you bring the photo of Terry?"

He pulled a dog-eared Polaroid from his shirt pocket and handed it to her. Although the woman wore a Carnival mask, Kate recognized her as the patient she'd known as Mary Johnson.

"She's a striking woman," Kate observed, "and her daughter takes after her."

"If anyone can find her," Mitch said, "it's Dean. The Garretts recommended him highly—"

"Haven't had much luck so far," Dean said with an ironic laugh.

Mitch glanced from Dean to Kate and back to Dean again with a teasing grin. "Doesn't look like your luck's been all bad."

Dean pursed his lips and kept his eyes on the road. "You could say that, except I'm afraid I've spoiled my chances."

Kate tried to ignore their bantering, knowing Dean was referring to her, and refused to rise to his challenge.

"Why do you say that?" Mitch's tone was serious,

but Kate's peripheral vision picked up the twinkle in his eyes.

"She caught me red-handed," Dean said with a sad shake of his head.

"With another woman?" Mitch pretended outrage.

"Nope. With my hand in her...desk."

Kate burst out laughing in spite of herself. "Will you two stop?"

"You're right," Dean said solemnly. "It's not a laughing matter."

Mitch appeared truly contrite. "I just wanted to put Dean's break-in into perspective. He was only trying to help me find Terry, and he didn't do you any real harm."

Kate opened her mouth to reply, then clamped it shut. How was Mitch to know how badly Dean's deception had hurt her, how much his lies had dredged up the pain from her past? Just when she'd hoped she'd learned to trust again, he'd knocked the props out from under her. But if she shared how much he'd disappointed her, he'd know how much she cared, and she refused to give Dean that much power over her.

Not to a man she hadn't learned to trust.

Not to a man she might never be able to believe in.

"You're right." Her airy voice contrasted sharply with the heaviness in her heart. "Dean didn't do me any harm. And I'm hoping he'll find Hope's mother for you soon."

Later, after an hour spent in the San Antonio police department, where every uniformed cop and detective she'd met had sung Dean's praises to the heavens, her emotions seemed more confused than ever. Okay, so Dean Harding was an all right guy, defender of justice and the American way, but did that ensure he wouldn't break her heart with more deception?

What she needed was time and distance from the irresistible cowboy. How could she be objective and think clearly when her pulse galloped like cattle in a stampede every time he was near her?

With a sigh, she realized she held the key to removing him from her life, perhaps for good. All she had to do was give him Terry Monteverde's last known Austin address.

AFTER LEAVING San Antonio, they dropped Mitch at the Double G and picked up Mikey, who chattered all the way home to Austin about the terrific time he'd had riding a pony and helping to curry a colt. His adventures, however, had worn the little guy out. Before Shelley had served dessert at supper, Mikey, with his head resting on his arm on the table, was sound asleep.

Dean pushed away from the table and gathered the boy in his arms. "He's all tuckered out. I'll carry him to bed."

Kate stood, tossed her napkin on the table, and glared at him like a lioness protecting her cub. "I can take him."

"I don't mind." Dean bit back the desire to say more. Why was every move a challenge with this woman? "He's quite a load to wrestle up two flights of stairs."

She started to protest, then set her mouth in a fine line. "I'll turn down his bed."

He followed her from the dining room, noting the agitation in her step. She'd been edgier than a scared pup in a lightning storm ever since their return from San Antonio. And distant and cool as a snow-capped mountain, as if the passion they'd shared had never happened.

With a sigh, he hefted the boy in his arms, enjoying the warmth of his slight weight against his chest, the little boy scent mixed with horses, hay and dust of the Double G, and the angelic beauty of his face in repose, still chubby with baby fat. Longing for a son like Mikey caught him unawares, and he blinked back telltale moisture from his eyes.

In Mikey's room, Kate had already turned down the covers, and Dean lowered the boy to the bed. He watched Kate strip Mikey's shoes, socks and clothes down to his underwear, then tuck the sheet around him. The maternal love radiating from her as she kissed her son good-night made her even more beautiful, more desirable.

Made him realize anew how unattainable she was.

Loss stabbed at him as if his heart were tangled in barbed wire. He'd blown his chances with Kate by not being honest with her. The respect the Garretts and his former colleagues in San Antonio had shown him had done nothing to soften her disapproval.

He thought of Luis Jimenez and his Catholic beliefs

and lamented his own lack of faith. Now would be the perfect time to pray to Saint Jude, the patron saint of lost causes. From the tight lines of Kate's face and her refusal to meet his gaze, only divine intervention was likely to bring him into her good graces again.

Leaving a tiny night-light burning, she left Mikey's room and hurried down the stairs. In the second-floor hallway, she turned to face Dean, who'd followed her. "I've decided to give you what you want."

At first, still gripped by his own longing, Dean misunderstood, but her pinched and angry look quickly convinced him she wasn't talking about affection, but Terry Monteverde's address. "Why now?"

"Because you've turned our lives upside down," she said without meeting his gaze, focusing her blazing eyes on a point past his shoulder. "Once you have what you came for, you can leave."

God, he'd hurt her even worse than he'd suspected. Pain emanated from her like rays from the sun. He searched for words to ease her bitterness, but couldn't find them.

"I'm sorry," was all he could muster.

She continued to avoid his gaze, her chin jutting at a brave angle of defiance. "If I can help you find Terry before whoever's trying to harm her, I'd like to help."

"I understand. Thank you." He jammed his hands in his pockets to keep from reaching for her.

"While she was in Austin, she stayed at what used to be a motor court out past the university. It's been turned into efficiency apartments called the Texas Rose.''

Dean nodded. He'd learned what he'd come for, but instead of satisfaction, he felt bereaved, as if someone had died. "Will you come with me while I check it out?"

She shook her head. "You have the address and your sketches of Terry. You don't need me."

God, was she ever wrong. At that moment, he'd never needed anyone so much in his whole life, and his only option was to turn and walk away.

"I'll drive out there," he said, "then come back here for my things."

At least returning would give him the chance to see her one more time. Maybe, if a miracle struck, he could think of a way in the meantime to win back her trust.

"Suit yourself." Continuing to avoid his eyes, she turned on her heel and hastened down the stairs to the first floor, leaving him alone with his misery.

A soft woof reminded him he wasn't entirely alone.

"C'mon, girl," Dean called to Bear. "Let's go for a ride."

Instead of twirling in circles and bounding for the door at the mention of her favorite pastime, Bear sidled next to him and licked his hand. He ruffled her fur, glad for the comfort, and headed for his truck, his heart heavy with loss, his mind whirling futilely in search of a solution to his dilemma.

IN LESS THAN twenty minutes, he was knocking at the office door of the Texas Rose Apartments, a conglomeration of tiny cottages built in the forties and in obvious need of repairs. An elderly man with a grizzled, three-day beard and a beer gut barely covered by a tightly stretched T-shirt answered the door.

"Can't you read the sign?" he snarled. "No solicitors."

Dean introduced himself. "I'm a private investigator."

The old man shook his head. "I run a clean place here, no hanky-panky—"

"I'm looking for a missing person. A Mary Johnson who lived here several months ago."

The man raked his fingers through greasy hair and shook his head. "My renters come and go. I can't keep up with them, and I don't remember any Mary Johnson."

"She was pregnant when she arrived. Had a baby girl while she was living here." Dean pulled a copy of the sketch from his pocket and handed it to the man.

The manager's eyes widened in recognition. "Yeah, I remember her. A classy dame. Didn't look like she belonged in a joint like this. But she's been gone for months."

"Did she leave a forwarding address?" Dean held his breath. If the man couldn't help him, Terry's trail would be completely cold. She could be anywhere on the face of the earth, a hell of a parameter for a search.

"Naw," the man said with confidence, "my renters never leave—"

"What?" Dean had caught the glimmer of remembrance in the man's bleary eyes.

"I remember this lady. She seemed real worried about somebody following her." His eyes narrowed, and his expression turned suspicious. "How do I know you ain't who she was worried about?"

Dean handed him his business card. "You can check me out with Detective Marston of the Austin PD. He'll vouch for me."

The man studied the card for a moment, then shrugged. "If you say so. She's been gone so long she could be anywhere by now."

"Did she say where she was headed when she left?" Dean prodded.

"Not exactly. But she said if any mail came for her, I could send it care of general delivery in San Antonio."

San Antonio?

Had Terry Monteverde been right under their noses all along? Or had she simply stopped off long enough to deliver Hope to Mitch and then moved on to God knew where? Dean had only one way of finding out. To keep looking.

"Thanks for your help." Dean turned toward his truck.

"Wait," the man called. "One other thing."

"Yeah?" Dean paused, hoping for a clue to narrow his search.

"Ever considered selling that dog?"

Dean glanced at Bear, sitting placidly at his side. "Never."

The man shrugged. "Good-looking animal. Doesn't hurt to ask."

Dean climbed into his pickup and started the engine. The office manager had pointed him toward San Antonio in his search for Terry Monteverde, but Dean wouldn't be surprised to find a dead end in that city. After assuring herself that Hope was safe with Mitch, the woman was probably long gone.

Even more depressing than his cold trail was the prospect of leaving Austin and Kate Purvis. With a heavy heart, he turned the truck toward the boarding-house. As much as he wanted to see Kate again, maybe the kindest move for both of them would be to escape without any awkward goodbyes. He intended to slip in and out without encountering anyone, if possible.

No such luck.

When Dean reached Shelley's Victorian house, a police cruiser and an unmarked car stood at the curb, a sure sign of trouble. Dean parked down the street with a squeal of brakes and tires, jumped from the cab, and sprinted toward the house, Bear close at his heels.

He took the front steps three at a time, threw open the screen door, and rushed into the hall. A mumble of voices led him to the front parlor. Shelley, pale-faced and trembling, sat on the sofa with Felicity beside her, gripping her hands. Detective Marston sat in a chair across from them, his expression grim.

"What's happened?" Dean demanded. "Where's Kate?"

Shelley tried to speak, but sobbed instead. Even the unflappable Felicity appeared at a loss for words.

Marston unfolded his tall frame from the chair. "Hello, again, Dean. You seem to follow trouble lately."

"Where's Kate?" Dean repeated.

"Upstairs," Marston said, "checking on her son, but don't worry. A uniformed officer is with her."

The muscles in Dean's jaw tightened, and he struggled to hold his temper. Blowing his top wouldn't get him straight answers any faster. "Will somebody please tell me what the hell is going on?"

Shelley gasped for breath and blurted, "It's Kate and Mikey."

"What about them?"

"He's going to kill them," Shelley sobbed.

Dean looked to Marston in confusion. "Who?"

"That," Marston said with infinite patience, "is what we're trying to find out."

CHAPTER TWELVE

"I THOUGHT YOU'D GONE."

Dean turned to find Kate standing in the parlor doorway. He flinched at her accusatory tone. "I intended to be, but when I saw the police cars—"

"They're none of your concern." The hurt in her eyes reproached him. She obviously didn't want his help. She didn't trust him, even when she and Mikey were in danger. Probably *especially* when she and Mikey were in danger. After all, from her point of view, he'd brought her nothing but trouble since they'd met.

Marston shook his head at Kate's declaration. "Ah, Dr. Purvis, that's where you're wrong. This affair is very much Dean's concern."

Dean slapped his thigh with his Stetson and spoke between teeth gritted in frustration. "Will someone please tell me what's going on?"

Tight-lipped, Kate slumped against the doorjamb and crossed her arms over her chest. The fatigue evident in the sag of her body and the fear glittering in her dark eyes made him long to go to her, to take her in his arms and shelter her from whatever danger threatened.

Fat lot of good that would do, he reminded himself, and held his place, because the set of her mouth and her body language repelled him as effectively as words. Since finding him in her office and learning his true purpose in coming to her house, Kate had branded him persona non grata and made clear she wanted nothing more than to see the back of him.

Marston turned his attention back to Shelley. "Tell Dean what you told me, Mrs. Purvis. Don't leave out any details."

Shelley calmed visibly at the detective's soft, soothing words, wiped her eyes with a tissue, and took a deep breath. "I received a phone call—" she glanced at the clock on the mantel "—about an hour ago. The caller must have mistaken me for Kate, because he called me Dr. Purvis. I tried to correct him, but he screamed for me to shut up and listen."

Remembering, she shivered, and Kate hurried to her mother. She sat beside her and wrapped her arm around Shelley's shoulders, but seemed careful to avoid Dean's gaze.

After casting a watery but grateful smile at her daughter, Shelley continued. "The caller demanded that I tell him everything I knew about someone named Terry Monteverde. When I told him I'd never heard of her, he called me a liar—I've deleted the expletives." She shook her head, her lips forming a moue of disapproval. "The man had a filthy mouth. He said if I wanted to keep myself and my son alive, I'd better do as he said."

Dean sank into the nearest chair. His hunch that

someone else was after Terry Monteverde had proved true, but being right brought no satisfaction, especially when it placed Kate and Mikey in danger.

"He told me," Shelley said, "to write everything I knew about this Monteverde woman's whereabouts in red ink on an index card and post it on the bulletin board at the Wishy-Washy Coin Laundry—"

"That's two blocks over in a strip mall," Felicity explained. "Most of our boarders, as well as renters in nearby apartments, use it."

"Go on, Mrs. Purvis," Marston prodded.

Shelley's face crumpled, as if she were about to cry again, but she pulled herself together. "He said if I didn't post the information by tomorrow afternoon, he would kill me, thinking I was Kate, *and* Mikey. Then he hung up."

Marston glanced at Shelley with admiration. "In spite of her shock, Mrs. Purvis kept her wits about her. Dialed star-69 and copied the caller's phone number before she called us. We traced the number to a public phone in Zilker Park. Crime Scene Unit is there now pulling prints."

"Will somebody, please," Shelley begged, "tell me who Terry Monteverde is and why someone's threatening my daughter and grandson over her?"

Dean gave a thumbnail sketch of Terry, Mitch and Hope's story and his part in the investigation, then turned to Kate. "What do you intend to do about the phone call?"

"Ignore it. I refuse to be intimidated by threats."

Marston stroked his chin thoughtfully. "I'm not sure that's the wisest course."

"You're not suggesting I give him what he wants?" Kate asked in indignation.

"Of course not," the detective replied, "but you should take his threats seriously. After talking with Dean about Leo Hayes, I looked into his case. The man was a cold-blooded killer as well as a smuggler. He certainly intended to kill Terry Monteverde. And he wouldn't have hesitated to murder her friend if the Texas Ranger hadn't killed Hayes first in self-defense. If the caller is somehow connected to Hayes, he may be just as ruthless."

"Post a card at the Laundromat," Felicity suggested with a fierceness alien to her gentle nature, "but give the bastard false information. Serve him right to lead him on a wild-goose chase."

"Until he discovers he's been tricked," Dean said, "and comes back angrier than ever and eager for revenge." He thought for a moment. "But you could post the card and place the board under surveillance. Nab him when he reads it."

Felicity shook her head. "Won't work. I know that laundromat. Before we got our washer and dryer, I used the place myself. Always jam-packed with customers, and everybody reads the bulletin board. It's the only entertainment while waiting for your clothes to dry. You'd never pick the guy from the rest of the crowd."

Marston frowned. "I don't have the manpower to

place Kate and Mikey under round-the-clock protection—''

''I do,'' Dean said.

Marston raised an eyebrow. ''What are you suggesting?''

Dean kept his gaze on Kate. ''Kate, Mikey—and Shelley and Felicity—can stay at my ranch until we catch the guy who's making these threats.''

Kate bounded to her feet. ''I can't do that!''

''Why not?'' Dean asked.

''I have a medical practice. I can't desert my patients.''

His former distaste for doctors momentarily revived. ''Not even to protect your son?''

Kate's adamant expression turned to chagrin, and Dean guessed that her objection had less to do with her patients and more to do with her anger at him.

''Dean's right,'' Shelley said. ''You and Mikey can't risk staying here. Abby can find someone to cover for you. If no one except the people in this room know where you are, you'll be perfectly safe while the police search for this man.''

''And Luis and Jorge Jimenez can look after them if I have to leave the ranch to look for Terry Monteverde,'' Dean added. The prospect of Kate and Mikey in his house pleased him, and not just because he wanted them safe. He wanted them close for his own reasons.

''If we go,'' Kate said to her mother with a hint of panic in her voice, ''you and Felicity will come with us. I don't want you in danger, too.''

"Nonsense," Shelley said. "We have boarders. Who'd take care of them?"

Felicity chimed in. "My youngest brother just retired from the Army Special Forces. I'll ask him to come for a visit. He'll be all the protection we need."

Kate's eyes grew round with apprehension, and Dean wondered which she feared most, the death threats against her or being alone with him?

"If you'll pack your things," he said, "we can leave tonight."

She shook her head. "Whoever made the threat isn't expecting results until tomorrow. Mikey's already asleep. I don't want to disturb him tonight. We're all shell-shocked. He'll pick up on our distress if we rouse him now. Tomorrow morning we can take our time. Make him think we're going for an ordinary visit."

Marston nodded approval. "If you're going to be here tonight, Dean, everyone should be safe enough. I'll ask for extra patrols in the neighborhood until we nail this guy."

"I'll sleep with my door open," Dean said. "Nobody will get past Bear and me."

"Felicity," Shelley said, "you'd better sleep in the third-floor guest room until this blows over. There's safety in numbers."

Marston headed for the door. "Any more threats, you let me know. Meanwhile, we'll see what the crime scene unit turns up on that pay phone."

Dean walked the detective to his car. "Can someone tail us out of town tomorrow? Make sure we're not followed?''

"Sure. Give me a call when you're ready to leave." Marston handed him a card with his cell phone number, then peered at him through the deepening twilight. "Any idea who's making these threats?''

"I'd bet my boots it's the same person who broke into Kate's study and office. I'll ask Dylan and Lily to see what they can dig up on Hayes's old associates.''

"Any leads on Ms. Monteverde?''

"She went from here to San Antonio. I'll have to resume my search there.''

"Be careful. Whoever's on her trail may be following you, letting you do the work.''

"I've considered that. I'll ask the Jimenez family to move into the guest house at the ranch tomorrow. Like Shelley said, there's safety in numbers.''

Marston shook Dean's hand. "I hope so.''

Dean watched the detective drive away, then did a careful surveillance of the street and yard before entering the house. He'd hoped to have a chance to talk with Kate alone, but everyone, including Felicity, had retired to the third floor.

Everyone except the elusive Peter Tirrell. Dean met him at the foot of the stairs, headed for the kitchen.

"What's going on?" Peter's tone was cool. He apparently hadn't forgiven Dean for taking him down in that flying tackle at the bus stop. "Why were the cops here?''

Dean didn't want to spook Shelley's paying guests. Besides, the boarders were under no threat, so they had no need to know. "New detective," he said, "just following up on the break-in in Dr. Purvis's study."

Peter halted and pierced him with a watery-blue stare clouded with disbelief. "How come a simple break-in rates so much attention?"

Dean shrugged. "According to the cops, the Maitlands are hot stuff in this town. Kate works for them, therefore she also gets the royal treatment." He smiled, trying to be friendly. "The rest of us peons just have to make do."

Peter grinned back. "Ain't that the truth?"

With a soft whistle to Bear, who was nosing around under the dining table in search of errant crumbs, Dean climbed the stairs to bed.

DEAN HAD THEIR luggage loaded in the pickup as soon as breakfast was finished. Mikey, who'd shattered the Sunday morning quiet with whoops of delight when told of the upcoming visit, had pestered Kate to hurry. Now, standing on the porch, she was suddenly reluctant to leave her mother, knowing how upset Shelley had been by the anonymous caller's threats.

"I'll be fine," Shelley assured her, and indeed appeared more like her usual perky self after a night's sleep. "Felicity's brother's flight arrives after lunch, and he'll take good care of us. You just settle down with Dean and enjoy yourself."

The matchmaking gleam had driven the worry from Shelley's eyes, and if Kate hadn't witnessed her mother's terror the night before, she might have suspected Shelley of concocting the entire scenario to throw her daughter and her handsome cowboy boarder together.

"Mommy, let's go." Mikey tugged on her arm.

"Give Nana a kiss," Kate said.

Shelley bent down for a fleeting peck before Mikey leaped off the porch and raced to the truck, where Dean waited, narrow hips braced against the front fender. With his Stetson pulled low on his forehead, all Kate could see of his expression was the grim line of his mouth and the tight set of his jaw.

Face it, she told herself, *he's not looking forward to this any more than you are.*

Oh, yeah? an inner voice retorted. *You're as jumpy as a virgin bride departing for a honeymoon. Don't tell me you're not looking forward to several days in the hill country with the charming Dean Harding all to yourself.*

Shut up, she argued silently. *Whose side are you on?*

Your mother's, the voice replied with a naughty giggle.

"Kate, are you all right?" Shelley's voice interrupted her inner dialogue. "You looked like you blanked out for a minute."

Kate forced a smile and swiped her forearm across her face. "It's the heat, Mom. Gonna be a scorcher of a day."

The giggle sounded in her head again. *Scorcher, as in hot, hot, hot. That's your cowboy, Kate. Sizzling, sweltering, sultry, torrid—*

Unable to quell her rebellious thoughts, Kate kissed her mother. "I'll call you tonight," she shouted over her shoulder, and ran for the truck.

Fortunately, Mikey had already climbed inside, so when Dean opened the door for her, her son formed a safe barrier between her and the cowboy.

The truck pulled away from the curb, and Dean checked the rearview mirror. "Don't look now, but our escort just pulled out three houses back."

"We're being followed?" she asked in alarm, and with a quick glance at Mikey, instantly regretted her question.

Dean nodded. "Marston's men. No problem."

Mikey, lost in his own thoughts, was oblivious to their conversation. "You got horses, Dean?"

"A few. I'm more what they call a windshield rancher."

"What's that?"

"That means I travel around my ranch in my truck more than on horseback."

"But you *do* have horses?"

"Four, to be exact."

Even under the restraint of his seat belt, the boy managed to bounce with excitement. "Is your ranch as big as the Double G?"

His eyes flashing silver, Dean laughed, a pleasant sound like water over rocks, music to her ears. "Not even half as big. But big enough."

Mikey peppered Dean with questions through the entire length of Austin and out onto the highway, and Dean answered each one with easy grace. Other men, she realized with a start, wouldn't have patience with her boisterous son, but Dean appeared to enjoy the boy's pestering.

He'd make a good father. Her blasted inner voice had returned. If she hadn't known better, she'd fear she was schizophrenic.

He would make a terrific father, she agreed, *but he's not husband material. Can't trust him.*

You're trusting him with your life, with Mikey's life. Why can't you trust him with your heart?

Because he lied to me. I've had enough of lying men to last a lifetime. Don't need more.

Grow up. He explained why he misled you. And he's still here, offering to help. Give him a chance.

She tried to think of an appropriate retort, but she couldn't. Her inner voice was beginning to make sense.

With Mikey's constant chatter and Dean's easy replies, the trip on the highway seemed short. In no time, Dean was slowing the truck for the turn onto a side road.

"Is this it?" Mikey asked.

"This is it," Dean replied.

A simple metal gate was all that adorned the entrance to the ranch, and Kate found herself curious about what kind of place Dean owned. There were plenty of dirt farmers and small ranchers around. If his ranch was like theirs, she might find herself in cramped quarters, too close to Dean Harding for comfort.

"Bear," Dean called to the dog riding in the truck bed. "Open the gate."

Bear bounded from the truck, trotted to the gate, and bumped the latch loose with her nose. Tugging on a leather strap apparently tied to the gate for that purpose, she pulled the metal barrier open. Once Dean had driven the truck through, she pushed the gate shut, reset the latch and hopped back into the truck bed.

"Cool," Mikey said. "Bear's just like a dog on TV or in the movies."

They drove on through the rolling hill country.

"How many acres do you have?" she asked.

"Around a hundred. Enough that I can work myself with some help from Luis and Jorge Jimenez, who live nearby."

When the truck topped the crest of a knoll, Kate glanced across to the top of the next hill, which was crowned by an attractive ranch house. This was no dirt rancher's hovel, but a large, graceful home. Peace and tranquility flowed around her, and for a second, she experienced an almost mystical sensation of homecoming. With hard-headed practicality, she brushed the irrational emotion away.

The house sat on an east-west axis atop the hill, shaded by a grove of live oaks, its floor-to-ceiling windows open to the prevailing southeast breezes. Surrounded by wide, covered porches and topped with a gabled roof of galvanized steel, the house was built of earth-toned stones, their edges softened by time and the elements.

"It's beautiful," she said. "What kind of stone is that?"

"Lueders limestone," Dean said. "It's mined and milled in West Texas, near Abilene."

"The colors suit the terrain. The house looks as if it grew out of that hill."

"The white limestone used in hill country buildings is too glaring for my taste," Dean said.

Just when she figured she'd pegged the man, he caught her by surprise. And how did a former cop afford such an elegant house? "You designed this?"

"Had to, to get what I wanted."

"Do you always get what you want?"

He pulled his gaze from the road and met her eyes. "Not always, but I try. Aunt Carrie left me enough to afford the place I'd always dreamed of. I'm a lucky man."

"Who's that on the porch?" Mikey asked.

Flustered by the unspoken promise in Dean's storm-gray eyes, Kate looked to the house, where a plump Hispanic woman with nut-brown skin, jet-black hair, and a shy smile waited near the front door.

"Tomasina," Dean said. "She, her husband Luis and their son Jorge help out when I need them."

He drove the truck slowly up the circular drive that threaded through the live oaks and pulled to a stop in front of the porch.

"*Buenos días,* Señor Harding." Tomasina's smile broadened. "I have put away the groceries in your kitchen and made the beds with clean linens, as you asked.''

''*Gracias,* Tomasina, you're a treasure.'' He introduced Kate and Mikey. ''Are you settled in the guest house?''

''Almost.''

''Let me know if there's anything you need.''

''*Sí, señor.*'' She hurried down the steps and followed a path that disappeared behind the main house.

Dean parked the truck. ''Let's get your luggage inside, then I'll give you the grand tour.''

Kate climbed out of the pickup and stepped onto the porch. Don Juan ramblers, sizzling red in the sunlight, twined around the porch columns and clung beneath the eaves. Their spicy fragrance lay heavy on the humid morning air, and their scarlet color against deep-green leaves provided a pleasing contrast to the earthen tones of limestone. Dean knew his roses. That much of his story when they first met had been true.

When she turned to look behind her, the view took her breath away. To the west, live oaks provided shade, especially from a late-afternoon sun. To the east was a large lake, and to the north, hills and ravines as far as she could see. Pivoting, she glanced south, where rolling pastures dotted with cattle stretched toward the horizon.

The covered porch was a haven in itself. Large, sturdy rocking chairs, pots of hanging ferns and a cool stone floor that still held the night's chill. Stepping through the open double doors, she caught her breath at the appeal of the expansive, open living area. The great room had an immense stone fireplace to the right and a full kitchen to the left, and another set of double doors opposite the front ones opened onto a broad screened porch that overlooked the pastures.

Dean's stamp was all over the room, rustic yet somehow elegant. Crammed bookcases filled the spaces between the open studs, leather sofas framed the fireplace, and on the rough-planked coffee table between them stood a battered, enameled coffeepot filled with summer wildflowers and prairie grasses. Indian blankets draped across the sofas or fashioned into pillows provided brilliant splashes of color.

"Wow," Mikey said beside her. "Look at that."

She followed his gaze to a rifle hanging high above the mantel.

Dean entered, both hands filled with luggage. "That's an antique lever-action Winchester, the gun that won the West."

Kate wasn't pleased with Mikey's fascination. "You mustn't touch it. Remember the talk we had about guns?"

Mikey nodded solemnly, then turned back to Dean. "Ever shoot anybody with it?"

Dean grinned. "Killed a lot of tin cans. Knocked 'em right off a fence rail. Tell you what, if it's okay with your mom, I'll let you try plinking at a few cans while you're here—"

"I don't know—" Kate began.

"But otherwise," Dean said sternly, "you're not to touch that gun or any other weapon without a grown-up's permission and supervision. Understood?''

"Yes, sir.''

A shiver of misgiving passed through her, not so much concerning the gun as Mikey's obvious hero worship. Her son had already decided that Dean Harding hung the moon. They would be his guests for several days, and Kate knew that leaving Dean would be hard for Mikey. He had never had a male role model, and he'd latched on to Dean like a thirsty man to water.

Admit it. You're not looking forward to leaving him yourself.

This time she didn't argue with her inner voice.

"I'll take your bags to your rooms upstairs,'' Dean said. "There's a bathroom down that hall—'' he pointed to the right "—if you want to freshen up before we tour the ranch.''

Dean disappeared down a hallway to the left, and Kate could hear the tread of his boots on the stairs. She sank into a corner of one of the leather sofas, still mesmerized by the attractiveness of the room. She shouldn't have been surprised that Dean had good taste and a sense of style. Her feeling of coming home had returned, as if she'd finally reached a place she'd been traveling toward all her life, and this time she couldn't shake the sensation.

"Neat place, huh, Mom?''

"Uh-huh,'' she replied absently. From the scars of his boots on the coffee table to the books in the bookcases to the Western art that graced the walls, the room was definitely Dean's. With the smell of leather, sunshine and the fresh Texas air blowing through the windows, the house even carried his scent. She was surrounded, embraced, not only by the house but by the man.

How, in heaven's name, in a setting like this, would she manage to keep her distance for the next few days? With a jolt, she realized that distance was the last thing she wanted. Her anger had dissipated, replaced by a longing she couldn't deny. Didn't want to.

Probably, she realized, she could whip her anger back into flames if she tried. But what was the point? Dean had confessed to his deception and apologized. Like a sulking teenager, she could continue to drive a wedge between them and never see him again after the police caught her anonymous caller. Or she could allow the adult in her to admit Dean Harding was a man she wanted to spend the rest of her life with. Seeing how he lived, discovering his hidden interests and talents had made her aware they had more in common than she'd ever imagined. He was perfect for Mikey. But, most of all, she'd never reacted either physically or emotionally to any man as she had to Dean.

Admit it, she told herself. *You love him.*

About time you recognized it, her inner voice replied. *Now all you have to do is tell him so.*

CHAPTER THIRTEEN

DEAN PLACED the last dish from supper in the dishwasher and glanced up just as Kate entered the room. "Mikey settled?"

She nodded. "He was asleep before his head hit the pillow. Between target practice, swimming in the lake and horseback riding, he's had quite a day."

Watching her curl into the corner of his sofa before the fire of mesquite logs, he felt a tightening in his groin and an ache in his heart. After Maggie's death, he'd believed he'd never find love again, but he was discovering that Fate always had a few tricks up her sleeve. Here in the house he'd labored to build and where he had intended to spend the rest of his days, solitary and celibate, sat the woman of his dreams.

Only one problem. Kate Purvis didn't trust him as far as she could spit.

With a sigh, he yanked the carafe from the coffee-maker and filled two earthenware mugs with the freshly brewed beverage. He had enjoyed the past few days with Kate as a captive audience. They had spent those days keeping Mikey entertained with horseback riding, swimming, and games on the sweeping back lawn, but Dean had treasured most the long summer evenings after Mikey had gone to bed. He and Kate had sat for hours either on the screened back porch or in front of the fire in the living room, sharing long conversations about everything from roses to books they'd read. Each evening they had found more common ground, more shared interests, more simple pleasure in each other's company.

He dared to hope she'd forgiven him for his earlier deception. He hadn't tried to kiss her again, but he remembered too well her responses from the times that he had in Austin. He knew she'd wanted him as much as he'd wanted her. But he also knew the disappointments of her past had left lesions on her heart.

He crossed to the sofa, handed her a mug, then sat opposite her where he could savor the sight of wind-tossed hair and cheeks reddened by a day in the fresh air. They'd laughed and played with Mikey, trying to forget the death threats of the anonymous caller that had driven Kate and Mikey into the sanctuary of his home.

He settled deeper into the comfortable depths of the sofa and sipped his coffee. "I haven't told you what I learned at the Texas Rose apartments."

"Any luck?"

He shook his head. "The trail is cold. The manager said Terry asked for any mail to be forwarded to general delivery in San Antonio, but that was months ago. She could be anywhere by now."

"I don't think so."

"Is there something about Terry Monteverde you haven't told me?"

Kate frowned. "Since the threats to Mikey and me, I've been worried about her. Someone particularly nasty is on her trail, and I'm worried now he'll find her before you do."

His anger surged. "You know where she is?"

"Not for certain, but I have a pretty good idea."

He couldn't keep the sarcasm from his voice. "Mind sharing?"

She lifted her head and met his gaze, her brown eyes earnest, her delicate eyebrows knotted in concern. "You're a good investigator. I'm amazed at the trail you've uncovered. But I have one advantage over you."

He pulled his mouth into a wry grin and struggled with contrary emotions. At the moment he couldn't be sure whether he wanted to kiss her or kill her for holding out on him. "An advantage such as knowing where she is?"

Kate shook her head, rustling the tendrils of golden-brown hair that framed her face. "I have a mother's instincts."

His hopes at a sure clue to Terry's whereabouts dwindled. "What's a mother's instinct got to do with this? She deserted her child."

"Did she?" Kate arched an eyebrow and considered him with an inquisitive look. "Or did she simply leave Hope where she knew she'd be safe?"

"What difference does it make?" Kate was frustrating the hell out of him, both mentally and physically.

"A great deal." Kate leaned toward him, her slender fingers gripped tightly around the mug. For the first time, he felt envy for a piece of pottery. "If Terry deserted Hope, as you claim, then the woman is long gone. She might even have returned to Brazil. But I don't think so."

"Okay, Sherlock, where do you think she is?"

"Mitch and Hope are living in San Antonio, right?"

"Right."

"That's where you'll find Terry."

Dean leaned back in his seat, digesting what she'd said, but still dubious. "I don't know. Staying near Hope would be a big risk."

"You don't understand. It's that mother's intuition I was talking about. If I had to place Mikey somewhere away from me for his safety, I couldn't bear not being close enough to at least check on him, to assure myself that he was being loved and properly cared for. The same's probably true for Terry, especially when Hope's so little and helpless. Terry loves that child. I doubt she could abandon her entirely."

Kate seemed so sure of her theory, Dean couldn't help weighing its merits. "There's one good way to find out."

He reached for the phone, punched in the San Antonio police department number and spoke with the desk sergeant. After hearing Dean's brief explanation, the sergeant agreed to hand out the artist's sketches of Terry Monteverde with a BOLO, a be-on-the-lookout alert, to the next three shifts.

"If she's in San Antonio," Dean said, replacing

the receiver, "sooner or later, the police will spot her."

Kate nodded. "What about the man who's after her, the one who threatened Mikey and me?"

"I spoke with Dylan Garrett while you were putting Mikey to bed. His man in Rio picked up Raoul Davega's trail. We can rule him out as a suspect."

"Why?"

"He doesn't live in Rio but a tiny village fifty miles away. He went home to see his grandmother. She took seriously ill unexpectedly. According to Dylan's man in Brazil, Raoul reached her before she died. He's staying now for the funeral."

"So we don't have any idea who made the threatening calls?"

"No more than we did on Sunday," Dean told her.

The police had found some solid prints on the pay phone where the call was placed, but Marston and his partner had ruled out most of them as viable suspects. The Laundromat had been placed under surveillance, but as Felicity said, the place was an anthill—it seemed as if everybody in Austin did their wash there.

Kate smiled, and the beauty of it took his breath away. "Looks like you're stuck with us for a few more days."

"I'd like sticking with you a lot longer than that."

The blush that had endeared her to him the first day they met worked its way up her cheeks. "I hope Mikey and I aren't going to be too much trouble."

"He's a great kid. I like having him here. You're both welcome for as long as you want to stay."

"I appreciate your kindness—"

"It's not kindness." He set his mug on the coffee table and pushed to his feet. "It's selfishness."

He took her mug from her hands, set it aside, and pulled her to him. Wrapping his arms around her, he gazed into her upturned face. For a moment, all he could feel was regret. Regret that he had drawn her and Mikey into danger, regret that his lies had hurt her, regret that she would never trust him...

With a jolt, he realized that she hadn't pulled away. A seductive smile tugged at the corners of her lips, and amusement twinkled in her eyes. She raised her slender arms and encircled his neck, her agile fingers stroking his nape, heating his blood. The gesture pulled her tight against him, crushing her firm breasts to his chest, molding her thighs to his. She couldn't mistake the evidence of his desire bulging against her pelvis, but it didn't seem to deter her.

Stunned, elated, he searched for words, but couldn't find them. In frustration, he shook his head. "I'm sorry—"

She stiffened in his embrace. Her smile vanished, and she tried to pull away. "I thought you wanted me."

"No, I—"

"No?" Hurt clouded her eyes, and she would have broken free if he hadn't tightened his grip.

He held on for dear life, fearing if he lost her now, he'd never have another chance. "Don't twist my words."

Her brown eyes flashed with golden sparks, and she

tossed her head like an agitated filly. "What's there to twist? There isn't any part of *no* that I don't understand."

"You didn't let me finish my sentence."

She relaxed slightly, but her expression remained wary. "I'm listening."

"I'm sorry for hurting you. That's what I was trying to say."

"And I misread your apology for something else?"

"No—"

"There's that word again," she said with a sigh.

From the set of her mouth and the squint in her eyes, he couldn't tell if she was teasing or serious. He had to guess right. Too much was riding on his response.

"I apologize for hurting you with the lies I told," he said, "but I don't apologize for wanting you more than any woman I've ever met."

Her slow smile returned, and she cuddled against him. "Then I was right."

He returned her grin. "Does being right turn you on?"

"No—"

"Let's make a pact. Neither of us can say *no* for the rest of the evening."

She leaned back to study his face, her eyebrows lifted in amusement. "Isn't that a bit reckless?"

His grin widened. "Exactly."

"As I was about to say, before you interrupted—"

"Me, interrupt?"

"Smart-ass. Maybe I shouldn't tell you."

If you could die from happiness and longing, he thought, he'd be a good candidate this very minute. Having Kate in his arms, in his home, in his life was a dream come true after a long, lonely nightmare. "What shouldn't you tell me?"

"That just being close to you turns me on."

"Then maybe we should get a little closer."

She glanced down. "Not possible."

He laughed. "And I thought you were a doctor."

She batted her eyes wickedly. "Well, maybe if we removed some of these clothes—"

He had all the incentive he needed. His mouth, hot and hungry, claimed hers, and his fingers skimmed the front of her blouse, shedding buttons as he jerked it from her waistband and shoved it off her shoulders. With equal frenzy, she attacked his shirt. Within minutes, their lips still locked in a fierce clinch, they stripped each other of every fiber of clothing.

He lifted his head for air and stepped back, admiring the play of the soft Texas twilight across her bare skin. "You're even more beautiful than I expected."

He skimmed his fingers down her arms, clasped her hands and drew her arms around him. The shock of her skin against his only increased his passion. He nibbled her earlobe. "I want to make love to you."

She threw back her head and laughed. "I thought you'd never ask."

With a groan of pleasure, he lifted her in his arms and laid her on the butter-soft leather of the sofa. His hands cupped her breasts and her body arched beneath him. Moans of delight escaped her.

He trailed kisses down the soft curve of her stomach, then settled himself between her legs.

Suddenly, she jerked upright. "No!"

Feeling as if he'd been felled by a pole ax, he drew back in disbelief. "No?"

She caressed his cheek. "Sorry—"

"You tease me this far, then stop, and all you can say is *sorry?*"

She cupped his face in her hands. "I shouldn't have used those words."

Propped above her on his elbows, he raised an eyebrow. "Which words?"

"*No* and *sorry*. They caused us problems a few minutes ago."

Struggling to understand, he asked, "What words should you have used?"

"How about *protection* or *birth control?*"

With a frustrated moan, he rolled off her to sit on the floor beside the sofa. "I don't have anything. I didn't think I'd need it. I'm amazed you're even speaking to me, much less—" He gestured to their naked bodies.

Her eyes mirrored his frustration. "My mother taught me always to finish what I start."

He reached for her and drew her close. "And medical school? What did it teach you?"

She threw her arms around him and kissed him hard on the lips. "Medical school. That's it! You're a genius!"

He eyed her skeptically. "What you have in mind won't be too clinical, will it?"

Disengaging herself from his embrace, she shoved to her feet, giving him a delightfully provocative view of her very attractive derriere. "My medical bag is upstairs. I always carry sample condoms in it."

"And you're going after it buck naked? What if you wake up Mikey?"

She tugged an Indian blanket from the back of the sofa and whipped it around her. "I'll be right back."

"Oh, no." He rose from the floor, grabbed a blanket from the other sofa and tucked it around his waist. "I'm going with you. If being close to me turns you on, too much distance might change your mind."

"Not a chance." She stretched on tiptoe and kissed the tip of his nose. "Race you upstairs."

Before he realized what she'd said, she took off running. Grateful that he lived alone so that no one would witness them wrapped in colorful blankets, running naked through the house, he followed her.

He burst into the second-floor guest room right behind her. Bent over her medical bag on the trunk at the foot of the bed, she rooted through it one-handed, then dropped her hold on the blanket to dig with both hands. The sight of her made his mouth go dry. Like a Greek goddess carved of honey-colored marble, the perfection of her slender torso, firm breasts and endless legs matched the beauty of her face. But she was more than a pretty package. She was the woman he loved.

With a victorious cry, Kate raised a foil packet in her hand, then clamped the other over her mouth. "I don't want to wake Mikey," she whispered.

Dean closed the door behind him, turned the lock and let his blanket drop to the floor. Her expression sobered as she watched him approach. She held out her arms to him.

With fierce tenderness, he laid her on the bed and slid beside her. "I love you, Kate."

"We've done too much talking already." She opened herself to him and pressed her mouth to his. Time stopped as he joined his body with hers, each stroke an agony of pleasure. With fierce tenderness, he drove deeper, until her cry of fulfillment shook the silence. He followed her over the edge.

KATE LAY IN Dean's arms, reluctant to move. Their lovemaking had been even more perfect than she had hoped, but she couldn't say she was without regrets. Moving slowly to keep from waking him, she sidled off the bed, covered herself with the Indian blanket once more and tiptoed from the room. Bear lay on guard in the hall outside the bedroom.

After a quick check on a soundly sleeping Mikey, she hurried down the stairs to the great room. In only a few minutes, she had tugged on her clothes and stepped out the front door onto the porch.

She didn't regret loving Dean. And she didn't regret their lovemaking. But she rued the fact that she hadn't considered where loving Dean Harding might lead. For every action, there was an equal and opposite reaction, but she hadn't yet figured out what her reaction to loving this man would be.

The scent of roses mixed with the perfume of night-blooming jasmine filled the air. Restless and unable to sleep, she decided a walk might help settle her thoughts—or at least make her drowsy. She could be safe enough if she remained in sight of the house. She stepped off the porch and ambled down the drive. In the distance, the plaintive call of a chuck-will's-widow split the silence.

She loved Dean, she admitted, but she also loved medicine. How could she live on Dean's ranch and still practice? Most babies would make their appearance long before she could arrive at the hospital from here.

She reached the bottom of the hill on which the house stood. Mikey, she assured herself, wouldn't be a problem. He adored Dean, and Dean obviously doted on her son. But how would her mother react if Kate and Mikey deserted her to live in the country? Shelley had already suffered a major disappointment over her divorce. Kate was loath to inflict more pain on the woman she loved most in the world.

Why isn't anything simple? she asked herself.

Nobody ever promised you simple. You have to take what life gives you.

"Stop right there, Dr. Purvis. You've saved me a trip to the house to find you."

Kate took a moment to realize that the last voice hadn't been part of her internal conversation. She halted on the drive and looked behind her, startled to see how far she had wandered from the ranch house while lost in thought. In front of her loomed a dark silhouette, and moonlight glinted off the chromed barrel of the gun he held.

"Now," the menacing but somehow familiar voice ordered, "you're going to tell me everything you know about Terry Monteverde."

CHAPTER FOURTEEN

HALF-ASLEEP, Dean reached for Kate. He'd told her twice tonight that he loved her, but he was still waiting to hear her say those words. Instead of the warm, naked Kate he was expecting, he found the other side of the bed empty. Instantly awake, he sat up and scanned the moonlit room.

She was gone.

He rose quickly, stepped into the hall where Bear was waiting, then peeked into Mikey's room.

No sign of Kate.

He clattered down the stairs, but the first floor was dark and empty, and Kate's clothes were no longer there. The hairs on the back of his neck stood on end as his cop's instincts kicked in.

Something was wrong.

After dressing with lightning speed, he lifted the Winchester from above the mantel, removed the bullets from the top shelf of the bookcase where he'd hidden them from Mikey, and loaded the rifle. On the porch, he scanned the countryside he knew better than his own face. Within seconds, he spotted her, trudging down the hill along the gravel drive.

He took a deep breath and made himself relax. She

wasn't leaving. She wouldn't desert Mikey. Maybe she liked to clear her thoughts with a late-night stroll. That was something he often did himself. With the rifle tucked in the crook of his arm, he started down the drive after her.

He'd sauntered only a few feet when his heart froze in his throat. A dark figure had stepped out of the shadows onto the road in front of Kate. Dean darted into the cover of scrub oaks and high grasses. Running at a crouch, he closed the distance between him and Kate in minutes. Moving silently, he managed to keep his presence secret until he was opposite the couple. Anger made his blood boil when he caught sight of the semiautomatic pistol the man trained squarely on Kate.

"I keep telling you," Kate was saying in a strong, unwavering tone, "Terry Monteverde left Austin months ago. I have no idea where she went."

"Don't jerk me around, Doc," the man said in a voice Dean recognized. "The private eye is on her trail, and he's tight with you."

Dean worked the lever action of the rifle, chambering a bullet with an ominous metallic rattle that broke the stillness, and stepped from the shadows. "Maybe I ought to blow you to kingdom come right here," he threatened. "And don't think I can't hit you before you even think about squeezing that trigger."

"Drop your gun, Peter," Kate begged. "You're not a killer."

With a start, Dean recognized the man. He was Peter Tirrell, Shelley's elusive boarder.

"How do you know I'm not a killer?" Peter snarled.

"Kate's a good judge of character," Dean said calmly, ready to fire if the man so much as blinked. "Leo Hayes might have been a cold-blooded murderer, but you don't seem the type."

"Who's Leo Hayes?" Peter asked, his gun still aimed at Kate.

"Isn't that who you're working for?" Dean asked.

"None of your damned business," Peter snapped.

The roar of a pickup in overdrive split the night. Headlights flared behind them, and Luis and Jorge arrived in a choking cloud of dust. The truck halted beside Dean, and the Jimenezes jumped from the cab, Luis with a shotgun, Jorge wielding a pitchfork.

"We saw you out with your gun," Luis said, "and thought you might need help."

At the sight of overwhelming odds, Peter dropped his arm. Dean closed in and confiscated the weapon. "Got a rope, Luis?"

His neighbor returned to his truck and grabbed a coiled lasso from the truck bed. He tossed it to Jorge, who trussed Peter's hands behind his back.

Dean rushed to Kate and placed his arm around her. "You okay?"

Even in the moonlight, the brilliance of her smile almost blew him away. "I am now."

Luis and Jorge manhandled Peter Tirrell into their pickup. "I will call the sheriff," Luis said. "You want a ride to the house?"

Dean glanced at Kate, who shook her head.

"No, thanks," he said. "We'll meet you there."

With their arms around each other, Dean and Kate turned back toward the ranch house. Her special lilac scent mingled pleasantly with the perfume of roses and jasmine, and remembering their lovemaking, he felt hot, even in the cool night air.

"Thanks for showing up when you did," Kate said. "I think most of his threats were bluster, but I couldn't be sure."

Thinking how close he'd come to losing her, he hugged her tighter against him as they walked.

"We've solved one mystery," Kate said. "We know now who made the threatening phone call."

"That means you're no longer in danger."

"You sound disappointed."

"I am. You and Mikey are safe, so you can go home now."

His house would seem emptier than ever, now that he had experienced how their presence had filled it. He'd had enough of loneliness and solitude. He wanted to wake every morning to see Kate in his bed, share winter evenings in front of the fire, hear her laughter and Mikey's ring through the rooms....

She stopped, cocked her head, and gazed up at him. "Are you trying to get rid of us?"

He groaned and grabbed her closer. "God, no. I'm trying to think of the right way to beg you to stay."

"For a visit?"

"Forever. Marry me, Kate."

If his unexpected proposal surprised him, it seemed

to stun her. She opened her mouth as if to speak, then shut it again and shook her head.

"Is that a *no?*" he asked, his hopes crushed.

She smiled at him and ran her fingers down his cheek. "That's an I-don't-know-what-to-say."

Relief surged through him. "You don't have to answer now."

"I'll sleep on it."

"Sleep on it with me?"

She grinned and headed up the drive. "I thought you'd never ask."

WITH THE SUN HIGH, Kate awoke to the happy yelps and laughter of Mikey and Bear playing in the front yard. She didn't know when Dean had risen, but no one, except Mikey, had gotten much sleep the night before.

After Luis and Jorge deposited Peter Tirrell in the great room, the county sheriff had arrived first. Dean had explained how and why Peter had threatened Kate and Mikey when Marston arrived from Austin. The detective's skilled interrogation revealed that Peter *had* intended to kidnap Mikey that day in the park, planning to hold him hostage for information about Terry Monteverde.

Neither Marston nor Dean, however, had been able to budge Peter from his story that he didn't know Leo Hayes. Tirrell refused to admit why he wanted to find Terry or if he was working for someone else. At last, in the wee hours of the morning, Marston returned to Austin with Tirrell in custody.

Dean had made long, languishing love to her before drifting off to sleep, but she had lain awake for hours, wrestling with his proposal of marriage. She loved him. She'd admitted that to herself the day before, but she couldn't see how she could fit her life—her practice, her mother and Mikey—into living at Dean's ranch. Next to her family, and now Dean, she loved medicine, and she wasn't ready to give it up. But she had no hope of maintaining a practice in the sparsely populated hill country.

She'd promised Dean she'd sleep on his proposal, but she was no closer to an answer than she'd been last night. She couldn't live without being a doctor, but she couldn't face life without Dean, either.

After a quick shower, she dressed hurriedly and went downstairs. The tantalizing aroma of fresh coffee greeted her, and Dean handed her a full mug when she entered the kitchen.

"Want breakfast or lunch?" he asked. "I've already fed Mikey both."

"Just toast, please."

She enjoyed watching a man who seemed so comfortable in a kitchen. He slid bread into the toaster, took butter and jelly from the refrigerator, and reached for a plate in an overhead cabinet. The sight of his muscles, stretching beneath the taut chambray of his shirt, brought back memories of their lovemaking and the sensation of his back muscles beneath her fingertips.

He turned, braced his hips against the counter, and

locked his gray laser gaze on her, jerking her from
her reverie. "Do you have an answer for me?"

"Answer for what?" She knew what he was asking, but she was stalling for time. Nothing had
changed since the night before. She loved him, but
she still hadn't figured out how to juggle her career
with being a rancher's wife.

He smiled, but she could read the uncertainty in his
eyes. "I asked you to marry me."

"I—"

Mercifully, the ring of the telephone interrupted
her, because she hadn't a clue how to respond to his
proposal. She *wanted* to marry him, but not if it meant
giving up medicine.

He reached for the extension phone by the refrigerator and listened for a few minutes to whoever was
on the line. When he replaced the receiver, he was
grinning, his marriage proposal momentarily forgotten. "A San Antonio cop thinks he's spotted Terry
Monteverde."

AN HOUR AND A HALF after the call from the San Antonio police, Dean drove his pickup through the out-
skirts of the city. Kate sat at his side, taking in the
sights. Since her move from Atlanta, she'd had little
time for sightseeing in Texas, and she was looking
forward to her first glimpse of the Alamo.

They'd left a very contented Mikey and Bear with
William Garrett at the Double G before heading into
town to check the identity of the woman the beat cop
thought was Terry. After cruising slowly past the Al-

amo for Kate to take a look, Dean parked near the Menger Hotel. They walked to the front of the building, where the uniformed officer waited for them.

Dean introduced himself and Kate. "What makes you so sure this woman is Terry Monteverde?"

The officer pulled a copy of the police artist's sketch from his pocket. "They handed these out when I came on duty this morning, and I recognized her instantly. For the past few months, she's always had lunch at the same coffee shop I do. Can't help noticing her. She's a good-looking woman."

"Know where we can find her?" Dean asked.

"After lunch today, I followed her here." The officer jerked his thumb to the hotel entrance. "She's always dressed in a maid's uniform. This must be where she works."

"I appreciate your help," Dean said. "We'll take it from here."

The officer touched his fingers to the brim of his cap and sauntered down the street.

"You think he's right?" Kate asked.

"Officers are trained to be good observers, but we won't know for sure until you get a look at her."

"If it's Terry, do you want me to talk to her?" Kate asked.

"No, she might get spooked and run if she knows she's been identified. We'll let Mitch make the first contact."

Kate tied a scarf over her head and put on a pair of sunglasses. "She probably won't recognize me in casual clothes. I'll tour the halls and see if I can spot her.''

Dean nodded. "I'll meet you in the Rough Riders Bar inside.''

They entered the hotel together, then split up for their separate destinations. Dean had just been served the beer he'd ordered when Kate returned.

Her eyes sparkled with excitement. "It's Terry. I saw her sorting linens in the second-floor corridor.''

A sigh of relief whooshed from his lungs. "Is she okay?''

Kate nodded. "She looks like she's lost weight and is probably working too hard, but otherwise she appears fine.''

"She didn't recognize you?''

Kate tugged off her scarf and sunglasses. "Didn't even give me a second glance.''

"You were right about her being in San Antonio, close to Hope,'' he admitted.

She gave him an I-told-you-so smile. "That's going to be some reunion with her and Hope and Mitch. Wish I could witness it.''

"I'll call Mitch now.'' He hurried to a pay phone in the lobby and dialed Mitch's number, but no one answered. Exasperated, he punched in the number of the Double G. Lily picked up the phone.

"We've found Terry,'' he told her, and filled in the details, "but I haven't been able to contact Mitch.''

"Nice work, Dean,'' Lily said, "and don't worry about Mitch. I'll call him, but not right away. Dylan and I want to keep Terry under surveillance for a while—figure out the best way to approach her without scaring her into hiding again.''

"I have a favor to ask," Dean said. "Would William mind keeping Mikey a little longer this afternoon? Kate and I have something else to take care of."

"Mind?" Lily said with a laugh. "You know how much Dad loves kids. You'd think he was still one himself. Take your time."

Dean thanked her and hung up. He was glad to have the Terry Monteverde case behind him. Now he could concentrate on more important issues. He'd noted Kate's hesitation when he'd brought up marriage again that morning, and he was pretty sure what had caused it. All the way into San Antonio, he'd been trying to think of a way around that obstacle, and he'd come up with what he considered a great idea.

Now all he had to do was sell Kate on his scheme.

KATE HAD HOPED to spend more time playing tourist in San Antonio, but when Dean returned from the phone in the lobby, he rushed her to the car.

"I promise," he said, "I'll bring you back for a full tour, from the River Walk to the Alamo—soon—but there's something else I want to show you first."

"Here?"

He shook his head. "You'll have to wait until we get there."

She was dying of curiosity, but her requests for hints went unheeded. Her interest only increased when they passed the entrance to the Double G without turning in.

"What about Mikey?" she asked.

"We'll come back for him shortly."

As he continued on the highway toward his own ranch, a suspicion niggled at her. "You're not hurrying home just to get me in the sack again, are you?"

"You're a mighty cynical woman," he said with mock censure, "although, now that you mention it, it's not a bad idea."

Laughing and feeling happier than she could remember, she smacked him on the arm. "Behave, and tell me where we're going."

They had reached the turnoff to Dean's ranch. He parked the truck at the closed gate. Kate waited for him to open the gate to drive through, but instead, when he climbed out, he circled the pickup and opened her door.

"We're here," he announced.

She jumped from the truck and glanced around. All she could see was pasture on one side of the road, rolling hills filled with scrub oaks on the other. "We're where?"

He held out his hand, his face creased in a devilish grin. "Come with me."

He opened the gate and led her through it and up to the top of a small hillock that overlooked the highway. "What do you think?"

"I think you've lost your mind. What am I supposed to be looking at?"

He opened his arms in a gesture that included the

hill where they stood all the way to the road. "You are standing on the future site of the Carrie Harding Memorial Free Clinic."

"What?"

Grabbing her hands, he pulled her close and wrapped his arms around her waist. "Do you love me, Kate?"

She gazed up at him in confusion. "Yes, I love you—"

"And will you marry me?"

Suddenly, she realized what he'd said earlier. "A free clinic?"

He nodded. "I haven't spent even half of the money Aunt Carrie left me. There's enough left to build a clinic and fund a foundation to pay for staff and operating expenses. We could build it here, where migrant workers and poor farmers and ranchers won't have to go all the way to San Antonio for treatment. You can practice medicine to your heart's content. And with so many young families, you'll have plenty of babies to deliver."

Her eyes filled with tears of happiness. She knew he loved her, but only now was she beginning to realize how much. "You'd do this for me?"

"For you, for us, for the people who need a free clinic. What do you think?"

"I think it's wonderful."

"Then you'll marry me?"

She hesitated, too overwhelmed to answer.

"If you're concerned about your mother, remember we have a guest house. She can visit any time, and we're not so far from Austin that you can't see her often."

"Yes," she said emphatically.

He paused and eyed her warily. "Yes what?"

"Yes, I'll marry you."

Dean let out a whoop that echoed across the hills, tossed his Stetson in the air, and lifted her off her feet to kiss her.

Several minutes later, when he came up for air, he tugged her back toward the truck. "We have to hurry."

"Where are we going this time?"

"To pick up Mikey. And to call your mother and Felicity. We're going to have a big family barbecue tonight, a special occasion to announce our engagement."

She didn't move.

"What's wrong?" he asked.

"Are you sure you want to do this?"

He swept her off her feet and swung her in a circle. "Kate, I've never been so sure of anything in my life."

Me, too, she thought, her heart brimming with happiness as she walked back to the truck with him. *Me, too.*

Silhouette **Romance**

Escape to a place where a kiss is still a kiss...
Feel the breathless connection...
Fall in love as though it were
the very first time...
Experience the power of love!

Come to where favorite authors——such as
Diana Palmer, Stella Bagwell,
Marie Ferrarella and many more——
deliver heart-warming romance and genuine
emotion, time after time after time....

Silhouette Romance——
stories straight from the heart!

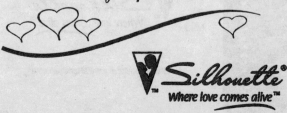

Silhouette®
Where love comes alive™

V *Silhouette*

SPECIAL EDITION™
Emotional, compelling stories that
capture the intensity of living,
loving and creating a family
in today's world.

V *Silhouette* ®

Desire.
A highly passionate,
emotionally powerful and
always provocative
read.

V *Silhouette* ®
Where love comes alive™

V *Silhouette*
INTIMATE MOMENTS™
A roller-coaster read that delivers
romantic thrills in a world of
suspense, adventure
and more.

Silhouette Romance
From first love to forever,
these love stories are for
today's woman with
traditional values.

Where love comes alive™

From first love to forever, these love stories are
for today's woman with traditional values.

A highly passionate, emotionally powerful
and always provocative read.

SPECIAL EDITION™

Emotional, compelling stories that capture the
intensity of living, loving and creating a family in
today's world.

INTIMATE MOMENTS™

A roller-coaster read that delivers romantic thrills
in a world of suspense, adventure and more.